Realm Of Domination

Sexy Stories Collection

VOLUME 34

11 EROTIC SHORT STORIES

PARKER HEIMANN

Realm Of Domination/ Parker Heimann. -- 1st
ed.
Xplicit Press, an imprint of TLM Media LLC

ISBN-13: 978-1-62327-565-5
ISBN-10: 1-62327-565-2
eISBN: 978-1-62327-615-7

Printed in the United States of America

CONTENTS

1 HOLDERS OF THE DEEP

As her consciousness slowly returned, Pamela tried to remember exactly what happened. Nearly everything was a blur. All she knew was that she was sinking further into the deep, dark waters.

Had she died? Her body was still feeling some sort of shock as if she was recovering from a tragic event. Something bad must have happened. Still, her body was intact; no limbs were broken. She didn't feel any bruises or scars although her body ached all over. Her mind felt sluggish and tired. God, she wondered, what could have made her feel this way?

A shipwreck. The thought popped in her head. Some images of being on a huge ship flashed in her mind. She remembered when the boat crashed into something, possibly some high rocks or wreckage, and started going down. Yes, that was it. She had been in a shipwreck. It was an accident. The captain of the boat was going the wrong way and-

Pamela looked up. The ocean's surface was so high up. She could hardly see light. Plus, she was breathing. This couldn't be right. She must have been dead, a ghost haunting the water's depths.

Her hands rubbed up against her skin. She rubbed her face, her arms, and even brushed her fingers in her silky hair. This could be no mistake. With such corporeal familiarity, that body she had known all of her life, she had to be alive.

Looking downward, Pamela saw a huge collection of rocks sitting on the ocean floor. They were emitting lights through some of the open spaces. Something was happening in there. She started to swim towards it. As she did, memories would periodically come back to her. Memories of the sea captain. The pirates. A painful life of being a slave, servicing the likes of human beings she hoped to never see again. Ending up in the depths of the ocean may have been a strange reward from a God that felt distant in Pamela's life for a long time. The old women always said that he worked mysteriously.

Suddenly, from the open holes of the rocks, Pamela saw some figures moving. They were like huge fish, flapping their tails gently behind them. They swam from the open holes and towards Pamela's direction. As they got closer and closer, Pamela realized that these beings could be no fish. These beings had humanoid features connected to their weird green fish tails flapping about in the waters. The closer they got, the more Pamela could make out their features, hair wavering over their heads, breasts out in the open as these creatures seemed unashamed. Women. They were all women, but none like Pamela had met before.

She heard of them in the pirate legends. Mermaids who had probably never worn clothes before, nude as the day they were born. They had a variety of skin tones, some as fair as the summer air, others as dark as the winter night. All of them were beautiful, unlike any human woman that Pamela had witnessed. Their heads were flowing with tresses of black hair, blond hair, brown hair, red, whipping delicately in the motions of the waves.

It was then that Pamela realized that she was naked, too. Shame flushed over her but the mermaids were around her just as quickly, brushing their hands on her. She saw that their eyes had gills, slit spaces for breath. It was so strange and bizarre. A strong, soothing force emanated from their hands. Each palm's energy felt similar, as if they all shared the same life force.

Don't be afraid, Pamela could feel the strange women saying energetically, without words. They wanted her to relax. Pamela's body started to ease calmly into a paralyzed trance as the mermaids held her, slowly exploring her body. They rubbed her sides, her face, and her breasts- instantly, her nipples hardened. Although Pamela couldn't be that physically responsive, she could feel everything.

Suddenly, a less pleasurable sensation entered Pamela's mind. A sharp tug of pain widened her eyes as memories started to flood her vision with familiar images. She could see the sea captain. Her heart opened. All the love she felt for him stirred to life. Clearly, he was right in front of her retinas, the sunset skies behind him. His face smiling. In a range of images, she saw herself in his bedroom once more. The heavy panting of sex and the hard rides of lap riding entered her memories again. His groaning and head turning, the seed spilling into Pamela's cunt- all of it warmed her up to the mermaids.

Moving in and out of memories and the present moment, Pamela would see the mermaids circling her body. The feeling of their hands as they lifted her limbs, explored her unprotected pussy and full ass- it did feel good. The memories made them better. She couldn't feel violated in any way. She didn't know what was going on, much less if she was really alive down here. For all she cared, she could have been in heaven or hell.

One of the mermaids dipped her hands into the pirate maiden's gaping cunt. There were no pretentions- these beings wanted to fuck her. Pamela had always thought of it unnatural to make love to a woman, though the pirate used to force her to sometimes.

Still, she had never been taken advantage of by women when she was physically unresponsive- only men.

Who could really consider these beings women, anyway? Their tails fluttered around the woman as one held her by her armpits, the others circling as a mermaid held her head to Pamela's lap. She was starting to eat her out. The mermaid's tongue was inhumanly long and wiggled in quite easily though it pressed against the walls with some friction. Pamela was moaning instantly. It felt so weird. She was afraid that the tongue would possibly crawl inside her like some sort of animal and get stuck deep inside of her. As the volume of her moaning increased, the visions slowly started to fade away.

Another mermaid crawled behind Pamela. With strong hands, it moved up and down Pamela's breasts, playing with her nipples. The mermaid held Pamela from behind, the woman's cunt still getting licked clean inside and out as a third mermaid helped the breast handler, pressing her lips against the nipples. Pamela felt her nipples suckled and kissed. Other mermaids would come up from time to time and kiss her against her skin. Nothing was off limits- her arms, her legs, her feet and toes even, were all getting attention from these oceanic creatures. They rubbed their hands against her body and brushed their breasts against her teasingly.

The Captain, Pamela wondered. What had happened to him? She missed him so. Would she find him down here?

Suddenly, one of the mermaids looked at Pamela and placed her hand over her face. The message was clear. Energetically, the mermaid wanted Pamela to forget the mortal world. Not only was the mermaid wanting her to forget it, she commanded Pamela to. A strong pulsing force cleared Pamela's mind.

Pamela watched as her memories started to fade into nothingness. Nothing existed here but the ocean and the mermaids.

They were still continuing their field day with her. Like scavengers over a three coarse meal, they were eating her out. The enigmatic creatures swapped Pamela's pussy around the circle, stuffing their tongues in deep, one by one. How unfair, the pirate woman thought. Pamela drearily wondered if these mermaids had cunts. How would they feel if a gang of humans swapped them around and fucked them for sport? Pamela's mind was trying to resist the trance, to feel some sort of emotion that could physically revive her bodily control. Be it elation or anger, she wanted to get excited. She wanted to move. All the same, what could she do? She could only take it. Her role in this circle of mermaids was to merely feed their sexual desires.

Her eyes spread out wide as she felt a tongue further than the other tongues in a quick motion. Pamela's orgasm came on with the sharp push. As juices sprayed out of her cunt and joined the surrounding waters, Pamela felt the tongue pull out slowly. Her ass was slapped playfully by one of the mermaids as she passed out.

Pamela woke up. She was lying on the ocean floor, still existing for lack of a better word. Lifting her head, Pamela looked over to her right. Towering tall, she could see the huge stack of rocks that the mermaids had come from earlier. The lights still glowed in their openings and cracks. Whatever happened in there, Pamela felt that she didn't want to find out.

Noticing that her arms could move, Pamela lifted her hands up in front of her face. She moved her fingers and tested their joints. She could move, the paralysis gone to an extent, although she still felt a bit groggy. Pamela placed her hands against the ocean floor. Lifting up a bit, she looked down at her legs. She was instantly confused. Her legs had been covered by a strange film that was very like seaweed, but not quite. Made of some interweaving substance, the film was binding her legs close together in a shape that resembled a tail. Where the mermaids trying to get her to look more like them?

Rubbing her hands against the material, Pamela's brows rose in surprise. The material had very much been seaweed, woven in a complicated manner around her legs and the bottom of her torso, ass and pussy included. At the same time, this regular seaweed was transforming into something else. It was becoming more fleshy and heavy, slowly thickening. The outside of it was slowly gaining some scales that could be flicked upward by the tips.

Frantic, Pamela bent down and attempted to rip some of the strangely woven tail. She didn't want to be like the mermaids. Nothing in her heart told her that life under the depths of the ocean could be better than life on the surface. Feeling a sharp pain move through her legs, she stopped instantly. This thing was becoming a part of her. Although it was very thin and she could see her legs through the transparent material, Pamela was heavily aware and frightened that this strange, newly formed appendix now shared a part of her body. Some shock also hit her as she noticed the film become more and more thick, second by second. It was a slow process, but soon enough, she was going to become like those mermaids. Pamela couldn't stomach the thought.

The woman tried to scream. It was a failed attempt. All that came out of the woman's mouth were bubbles as gargling sounds traveled from her throat. Pamela wished she could drown. That was when she realized that she could feel no breathing emanating from her nose or her mouth. She wasn't breathing at all, at least not from where she was used to breathing.

Rubbing her hands up and down her side, Pamela could feel them. Gills. With each natural rise and fall of her chest and ribs, the gills brought in oxygen naturally. As weird and freaky as it was to feel these strange changes affecting her body, Pamela felt a sense of curiosity. She was convinced that soon, she would be like the strange creatures she saw. Thoughts of escape filled her mind but, even as the trance had worn off significantly, Pamela felt as if something was holding her to the ocean floor. Something entertained the thought of magic in her mind. Yes, she was being held her magically. The mermaids had made that strange force they used pin her to the floor like a specimen awaiting experimentation.

Pamela's legs were melding. She could feel them as if they were melting and melding together, no longer visible in a developing fish tail that was no longer transparent. Several attempts to scream came naturally from Pamela's diaphragm and mouth. Only bubbles would rise. Her eyes ached, as she could no longer see the surface. Only water. Only ocean beds.

Pamela felt something shoot into her pussy that was no longer visible. Her ass and lap were melding with the tail, becoming a part of it, as the top of her torso underwent no physical changes at all. The human world would forever be gone to her. Pamela was sure of it. There would be no more pirate ship trips, no Caribbean travels or treasure pondering. The captain was probably dead. The crew didn't have a chance; they were all direction following fools that couldn't even execute orders properly. It was all their fault that Pamela had gotten into this mess in the first place. The woman suddenly felt regretful for her life as a pirate wench. If only things could get better from that point on.

Pamela heard movements. Looking up to the collection of rocks, Pamela could see the mermaids swimming carelessly with their hair flowing behind them. Great, just great. In the middle of Pamela's changing, the mermaids were coming to get more of their new sex toy.

The women circled overhead, looking down at Pamela. Pamela looked up at them, cautiously staying still. She didn't want to invoke their anger. So far, they had been pretty hospitable, even with the rape. If she played her cards right, she could eventually win them over. She may have even been able to convince them to let her go. Well, couldn't she?

The mermaids approached. Pamela could feel the magic around her becoming heavier, pressing her against the ground with little leeway. No longer could she raise her back or her limbs for that matter. She was pinned down like a woman on an inquisition table but without the aid of straps, bonds, or other restrictive devices. Fear rushed through her mind again as she tried not to think about the mermaids. Her mind tried to turn to memories. Memories of the Captain, the crew, the ship as it was hit, the screaming and wailing, the discovery of strange beings swimming near the ship, ripping it to shreds from the bottom-

They did it, Pamela realized as she looked at the mermaids with disgust. They destroyed our ship.

A hand pressed against Pamela's head and all of the memories disappeared once more.

One of the mermaids pressed her left nipple into Pamela's mouth as she held Pamela's head in her right hand. Pamela moaned against the breast, her back arched up with only the aid of the mermaids surrounding her. Other than her mouth, she was paralyzed. She licked and suckled the breast as if she was nursing on it. It tasted so nice against her lips and her tongue. More moans sounded from Pamela's lips as she felt two other mermaids grab her own breasts and give them a suckle. The two willing mermaids worked their lips and tongues against the woman's nipples, enjoying their hardness and perk feel.

At that moment, Pamela realized that her cunt didn't feel like it used to. Not when she was human. She had a new feeling. A strong, sexual energy shot from where her cunt used to be all the way down to her newly formed tail. She could tell that her tail had fully materialized now. No longer was it a hardened film of seaweed waiting to become something else. Like a caterpillar, the crystallization had finished, an extra appendix formed.

One of the mermaids laid on Pamela as the other mermaids backed up. Her fish tail rubbed closely and sensually against Pamela's. The woman's eyes looked directly into Pamela's eyes and, instantly, Pamela could see her dominance. She was the leader of this mermaid pack. Now, Pamela would recognize her as a leader without disobedience or defiance. Feeling the leader's energy radiate from her tail, Pamela became more relaxed and ready for her initiation.

The leader bent down and kissed Pamela deeply against the lips. Her lips were soft and teasing, her tongue inserting and pressed against hers playfully. Rubbing her hands against the leader's arms, Pamela wasn't shocked to see that she could move again.

Tanya is my name, the dominant woman vocalized from her mind.

Pamela's eyes widened. This woman could communicate in words? And in English, surprisingly. Pamela was used to seeing these seas swarming with Spanish ships, like her Captain's ship had been. He had kidnapped her years ago from her previous Captain, and that Captain had kidnapped her years before that.

Those troublesome memories are coming back, Tanya thought telepathically with amusement before kissing Pamela again. Pamela kissed the woman sensually, rubbing her back and pulling her close. Their tails brushed against each other as the scales lifted and fell playfully. The nipples of their breasts were hardened from the friction shared between them. It was all so intimate.

Pamela felt like she was in on a secret that the human could never know. Sure, there were many legends of the strange beings that inhabited the sea- mermaids, krakens, monstrous whales and even sea demons. This, however, would arouse the fears and disdain of the human world even more. Who would have known that the forbidden pleasures of the world that had been denied to the human population existed far under the sea without persecution? Pamela had never dreamed of being truly attracted to or turned on by a woman, yet here she was with her new leader. Although Pamela had loved many a Captain, she was often saddened by the strange acts of lesbianism they would force her into, especially her last one. For this woman and her pack, however, Pamela would do anything. She was willing to put her all into making this community see her as a loyal companion and sex partner.

You are a sister now, Tanya said as she brushed up and down on Pamela, her tail so close against the woman.

Sister, one of the mermaids said above them.

Sister, joined another.

All of them were joining in. Pamela felt tears rushing down her eyes as Tanya held her down, kissing her and massaging her tail. The word sister went from a floating telepathic thought moving around a circle to a unified, constant chant. Throughout the rest of the love making session, the mermaids continued to say the word over and over again. Sister, sister, sister... Pamela felt so invigorated.

As her newfound sexual energy was peaking, thoughts started to race quickly into Pamela's head. They were all thoughts that weren't hers. She was getting images, sounds and sensations of joy and pain. At one moment, she saw herself on a slave ship sailing from Africa with drunk Portuguese sailors torturing dark skinned women. In another, she was on a British colonial ship fleeing religious prosecution with her family, secretly beaten by her cruel husband. In another, she was a Spanish prostitute kidnapped by pirates, experiencing a fate that was very akin to hers. She quickly understood what was going on. The memories of her sisters were all flooding into her. They came from various parts of the world- Europe, Asia, Africa, and even the New World. Their tales were many, human lives that knew pleasure and pain, heaven and hell. How could she do nothing but relate to them all?

The last memory that flooded into her mind was the one of her new leader. She had always been here, a woman from a long line of sea people once vast with their own kingdom. Now, that kingdom had been reduced to nothing but a pile of rocks. Tanya was populating her own colony now- a colony of sea women. She would show them the way.

Her tail was filled with so much sexual energy as she rubbed it rapidly against her leader's tail. She felt as if she and Tanya were really bonding. She and Tanya were one.

At that moment, a great collection of juices shot from Tanya and Pamela's tail. They shared a strong and powerful orgasm. Pamela had never felt anything like it.

Understand, my sister, Tanya said telepathically as she stroked her hand through the new mermaid's hair. Understand that we did this to make you free. We did this because we love you.

Pamela nodded. Yes, she did understand. This was their new home. The women had all come here for a purpose, a reason. The human world was so cruel and harsh. A woman's life in the human world was even harder. Here, in the ocean, she could be free with her sisters. She could celebrate her womanhood, her true self.

Sleep, my dear, Tanya said as she kissed against Pamela's skin. Your new life has begun.

The other mermaids swam behind their leader as Pamela rested on the ocean floor, her transformation finished.

Pamela woke up. Her mind spun as she tried to gain her senses and recollected exactly what had happened.

She must have been knocked out. Had her Captain beat her again? He was such a barbarous person. How did she sink this far down? She looked up to see the surface and make a swim for it. No, she couldn't- her body was too weak, her legs and arms too weary. If only she could muster the strength to get back up.

When she looked down, she could see she was very close to the ocean floor. There was a huge collection of rocks and they were glowing from the gaps and crevices that lined them. Before long, she saw women rising out of the mound of stones, swimming to greet her.

2 ABYSS OF THE DEMONS 1

The air of the prison was rancid. Small brittle fragments of assorted debris were scattered upon the floor, nearly unbearable under Tasha's legs. What could she do? Nothing. Logic told her often that there was nothing she could do. Her mind was gripping to sanity like stale bread in the hands of a beggar. She complained, but there was no solace for a woman chained to a brick wall in the darkness, helplessly at the mercy of her captors. She had heavy and tight bracelets on her ankles and wrists. Those bracelets were attached to silver links hardly extending from the wall. Stuck in a small spot, Tasha had little room to move about – she might as well have been plastered into that cold corner.

She thought over the various things that she could do to get out of her predicament. Each idea proved to be utterly hopeless in a matter of seconds. She had once been a contortionist. Maybe she could slip her hands through the bracelets in a matter of seconds. No, she thought. That was utterly stupid. It hadn't worked in the past 3 weeks. Neither had her strong woman training. Those circus days were behind her, and the life of a prisoner may have been something she would have to get used to. She had been won fair and square; the captors fed her regularly with... a variety of things – at least she thought so. She never remembered when she ate or when she drank. There had to be some reason why she was still alive, why she had an idea that she could count the days. If she had really been neglected, she would have been dead by now.

Snap out of it, she thought to herself. Thinking was more of a torture than the confinement. One minute, she would think about escaping. The next minute, she was accepting, after an hour she had juggled so many thoughts that she would break into another cold sweat. What could they want with her? Why wouldn't they let her go home?

Won. She was a prize that had been won. On Earth, her last boss had been a ringmaster of the Calamity Circus. She always knew that he had been a devil, dining with nobles in every town and city they visited, gaining hatred from locals for stealing money. Now, he had sold her to strange beings with mysterious methods for trapping women. They couldn't have been human, though they masqueraded as humans in the beginning. Now, they gave no pretentious personalities to hide their real nature.

Suddenly, a bell rang loudly. The overhead light snapped on. That meant they were going to begin. From the cracks of the prison walls, puddles of a black inky substance flowed out and toward the center of the room. There were no doors to this room but this is how "they" came in, those amorphous beings that loved to toy with Tasha so.

The imprisoned woman squirmed frantically as her eyes opened, looking toward her visitors. She couldn't deal with this again. Here she was, a human woman with dirty olive skin and unkempt auburn hair, reeking, trembling with a frail body that had once been so voluptuous. Now, she was nothing but a broken-down slave.

Immediately, the amorphous beings formed into five humanoid shapes. By their forms, two of them seemed to be women and the other three were more masculine. They were still black as ink but shiny with no noticeable features past the outer contours of their bodies. They had no noses, eyes, mouths, or ears for that matter, but they did have a muscular definition. Energy emanated from them that possessed an edge both seductively appealing and repulsive.

The ringing of the bells ceased.

"Tasha," one of the male forms said as he looked at the woman like a new playmate, "you still haven't accepted your new form yet."

Tasha squirmed as she saw the five beings

approaching closer. She found their uniform blank features hideous. Even though they didn't have any eyes, she could feel their intense stares from their solidly empty faces, and she didn't like how they were looking at her.

"You will be free," one of the feminine forms said as she leaned the closest to Tanya's face. "Truly free." The dark being reached her shiny, slender black digits across Tanya's trembling cheeks before kissing the woman passionately on the lips.

From the kiss of that smooth kettle-toned face, Tasha's eyes opened wide. Her pupils, once a forest green dimmed by the prison light, flushed with black – pure black.

With what was left of Tasha's conscious mind, she could feel the dark being shoot some inky extension into her mouth like a tongue or some strange cock. By the time this extension had move beyond the woman's throat, she had already lost her usual sense, her conscious mind lost. Everything in her eyes, even the white surrounding her pupils, had turned into a complete black texture.

"Oh yes," the black rubbery entity moaned sexually.

Tasha was crying black tears as the extension traveled all the way down her body. The pressure of the entering gush of black was intense, sometimes hardening, seeming to move and flow through her blood, massaging organs, and working to become a part of her. It wasn't long before Tanya's body could feel the foreign darkness in her sex organs, polluting her ovaries and playing with sensations inside of her cunt from the inside.

"Oh! It's so warm," the pleasuring said. Its mouth lacking face wore the energy of a smile.

Tanya ached not only in her energy field, sexual organs, or body but all over. She was in pain – it was a deep and undeniable pain that dragged through her soul without end or warning. She could only grit her teeth and scratch her nails on the floor as this thing had its way with her. With her mind empty of thoughts and her human reasoning vanishing behind her walls of flesh, she couldn't really think indifferently to the sensations overwhelming her.

The dark beings were all groaning and making noises of interest that filled the room. The prison cell was draped with a rancid smell and scary air of isolation. The creepy vibes rising from the beings made the place even less sanitary.

A strange voice seemed to literally crawl out of Tasha's lips – the voice of some other half inside of her. "Push.... Push..."

Suddenly, the imprisoned woman's pussy gushed with black ink running from between her legs. The ink poured on the floor of the prison as the dark beings stood around, admiring the handiwork taking place.

"You are special, Tasha," another of the male forms said. "You are us."

"We are you," the other female form said as she watched her sister completely digging into Tasha's mouth with ravenous desire.

Tasha's body was moaning. The moans

started quietly but they were increasing. The dark inkblot of a woman moving around her was losing that humanoid shape with each tongue-like thrust in Tasha's wet mouth. She was pressed against the prisoner with a variety of newly formed ink limbs holding her down, pushing harder into her without mercy. There was no guilt, sadness, or worry as the ink being knew that Tasha's other self, her new side, her true inner being, liked it.

"You are demon. Accept this fate."

"I... am..." Tasha's black tears had already covered her face, neck, torso, and legs by now. The dark sister was melding with her body as well. It looked like some goo was feeding off of her, taking her inner essence and making it a gaping hole. Not only did it appear to be this way, but this was exactly what was happening. This was what had been happening the past 3 weeks. Slowly, Tasha's soul was being drained out, her new dark soul gaining ground. This was how such an initiation worked. Tasha had been won, and now she would be won over.

"We're such charmers," one of the men said before laughing profusely. The laughter was sinister – sadistic even.

From the moans, Tasha's laugh joined them too. No, it wasn't Tasha, couldn't be; it was something else, something with dark eyes, and something with skin that was turning black as well. It was a being whose form could become solid and strong but run as thick as blood. It was evil, filled with lust and desire.

Somewhere inside, what was left of a destroyed Tasha screamed.

"See?" the female hovering over Tasha said as she had already ripped off Tasha's clothes and digested them, playing with her tits, suckling her. "No more thoughts. No more fear. No more pain. You are not that human body. You are more. You are eternal." The being laughed as it ran its inky limbs through Tasha's runny cunt, asshole, and mouth. "We meld. We are one."

"You are us," another male being said.

"Bring us more!" said another.

Suddenly, the bell rang once again. The ink beings started to move away from Tasha as the woman slowly started to become fleshy, reverting back to her old self. It was a self that was slowly losing ground in the real world, a self that would be erased soon.

"Two more weeks, Tasha," the recoiling feminine being said as it dripped in black substance toward the cracks of the walls, disappearing.

"Two more weeks before you indoctrinate other prizes with us."

The others followed quickly, splashing into puddles and creeping through the walls. They were gone, those filthy creatures. Leaving the woman behind, she was already forming a more convincingly human shape, her auburn hair visible again as her eyes were closed, and her skin regaining that olive complexion. The overhead light dimmed. She was alone again, sleeping calmly in the darkness.

When she would woke up, she would

remember the dark figures, their strange energy, some words and a scary kiss, but after that, anything else would draw a blank. She had experienced it before, during her imprisonment, and there were would be more sessions to come before she would completely lose any form of her old identity in the next two weeks.

"The world is a scary place," Scarlet said as she washed her feet in the side of the river. Even the beautiful sunset over the horizon couldn't calm her fear down. She was a beautiful woman, pale and freckled, her light red hair long over her shoulders as her green dress rose over her knees.

"The world has always been this way," her suitor, Marc, said as he bent down and drank some of the water from the riverbank. He was a tall and brown-haired man with broad shoulders, his clothes fancy and opulent even for hunting gear. Who could expect less of a King? "It's funny how when people see a few bad things happen here and there, they suddenly live in some paralyzing state of fear."

Scarlet sighed and looked at the suitor with a look that showed a huge lack of entertainment. "There you go, speaking to me like I'm a child again. Listen, I know that scary things happen all the time. You just have to know that I'm not use to all of this."

Laughing, Marc stood up and backed

away from the water by a few inches. There was still blood on his pants, hands, face, and hair. He looked down to Scarlet's beautiful legs, tainted by dry blood with her now clean feet. "Well, welcome to my world."

Scarlet shook her head as she stood up. "I'm damaged goods now. Who would want to invest their time with a killer on the marriage market? I sure as hell don't want to marry you."

Marc stuffed his hands in his pocket, approaching Scarlet with a shrug, "It doesn't matter. You may be a grown woman. You may have your own village. Who cares? Your people are starving and your crops are not plentiful. I wager most of them hate you."

The woman folded her arms as she looked at the persuader, "So what, you're thinking you've got it sealed in the bag and that we should get married then?"

Marc sighed. "The truth of the matter is that your family is ready for you to make a better step in your life. Your father likes me. He's tired of you wasting away precious opportunities for his village to make money." Shrugging, the suitor smiled. He could tell by Scarlet's eyes how sexy she found it whenever he gave a little smirk. "Doesn't matter. What matters is that you are a killer now. I did not murder any of those people alone. You helped me and your hands are unclean because of it, too."

The woman shook her head, looking idly down at the Earth, a bit shaken. "You're cruel... I don't understand my attraction to you."

Marc bent down and kneeled over the woman, holding her chin and kissing her deeply. "Who understands the attractions within the mind, the heart, and the... fruit of our passions?" One of Marc's hands slid between the young maiden's legs. He could already tell that she was soft and fertile, waiting for another love session. "Look, Scarlet, I have been all over. I've done horrible things. I've gained many wives. They were all hesitant at first. But before I married them, or invested any money to their villages, parents, or homes, I let them know upfront who I am. I deal with strange and powerful people." Marc kissed Scarlet deeply and passionately with a flickering tongue before she continued. "They have seen and do things that would make you tremble, shiver... sure, your father is a chieftain. I respect him, admire him. Still, ownership is a business. I'm simply a more powerful businessman as a King. That is the simple truth."

Scarlet couldn't help but moan now. It was loud and abrupt. She had resisted from moaning the whole time that Marc had been speaking and fingering her at the same time, breathing heavily for personal restraint. After a while, she couldn't resist. It was hell but heaven at the same time.

Marc had been right in referring to Scarlet's cunt as fruit; the walls were nice, fat, and juicy like a peach. It stained his fingers instantly with a sweet and clean smell. For a village woman, Scarlet took care of herself. She smelled of lavender and rosemary. He liked it, inhaling her scent and digging into her like a farmer in springtime.

"You are a part of this now, my love. Stick with me and you will gain many fruits for your labors."

Scarlet's eyes closed in pleasure as Marc moved in on her, kissing her deeply, running a hand in her hair. She spread against the ground, feeling her legs rubbed. This was so strange but it really felt right. She trusted what Marc said even though she knew very little about him. All was still a mystery to her.

As her father told her, she could protest all she wanted, but King Marcus had won her fair and square.

Won.

Scarlet pulled away from Marc's lips though no other part of her body protested from his touching. "Even though we did that to the men... did we really have to do that... what we did... to the woman?"

Marc looked into Scarlet's eyes calmly. He didn't sigh with annoyance or grit his teeth out of anger. It always seemed like he was more patient with her when they were making love. "My dear, there are those who are winners and those who are losers. All are given their rightful reward and place in this strange life of errors and earnings. You shouldn't worry about her; she earned her fate."

As Marc moved his face closer to Scarlet's light visage, Scarlet's hands pressed against his chest and held him an inch away. "How many more men do what you do to women like that?"

"Many of us. It is the price of success."

"She just vanished into that dark void. What is her fate now? Is she dead? "

"Oh, no, she is not dead." Marc smiled sweetly. "Scarlet, anyone that wants to really be made in this world has to depend on the forces beyond our comprehension: they are the forces that guide us."

"Forces?"

"You'll understand."

Marc kissed her again, ignoring the little twists and turns her body made in resistance. He knew it was temporary as she was suddenly willing again; her legs spread open and her mouth pressed against his sweetly. Her smell drifted lightly in the natural air surrounding them. There, on that riverbank, with the sunset nearly over and forests surrounding them for miles on end, the new couple had a place to call their own for the night. With each thrust of fingers into Scarlet's now gaping vagina, he knew she would be ready.

"Oh. . ." Scarlet softly muttered.

Marc understood Scarlet's feelings of fear and resistance. He had an understanding of how his experiences would make her nervous, squeamish, and afraid of a lifestyle involving murder and deceit. Still, he couldn't help but enjoy the chase, the earning of wives, and sharing a joint world of corruption with them. All the things he had done for the demons, the dark amorphous beings, were way too heavy for him to hold for his own knowledge and comfort.

"Don't stop," Scarlet said as her spread legs kicked a little bit with Marc on top of her and his pants dropped. The fingers had left minutes ago; it was his dick doing his dirty work inside of her now. He laughed, wondering how her father would react if he knew they were having sex before any announcement of their marriage plans. Fuck it! He knew how desperate her people were for money. He had only married into other royal families a few times; it was good for cooperation between other kingdoms, allowing war to be avoided. At the same time, tribeswomen were way more fun. Their ways were simpler and he had to respect their chief families made up of hunters and priestesses. It gave him another world to explore.

Marc's thrusts into Scarlet were becoming harder, pulsing into her rudely as he held her arms and dug into her. She had screamed at moments, though he could tell that she was trying to suppress any loud voices. For a tribeswoman, she was so prudish and reserved. Did she think that they would be found bloodied and sex craved, easily questioned by a passerby? He was the King of these lands – even in the frontier, he was the ruler and no one could do anything.

His cock was soaked as it pressed into Scarlet. She was really hot inside. Pressing her against the ground, all of his contemplative thoughts breathed in the winds of sex and ceased instantly.

Scarlet, on the other hand, couldn't help

but think: think about the men they had ambushed in the carriage, think of the way her future husband held them up with a sword pointed right at them, and how he butchered them and forced Scarlet to butcher others with a spare knife. How that woman....

The woman had disappeared as soon as the King had pulled out the shiny black stone. Scarlet remembered the strange magenta glow emanating from the rock. One moment, you see a beautiful blonde standing before you in a flowing gown and tiara. The next, she was gone.

"Marc... ooh... was that woman... royalty?"

Marc was gritting his teeth from rough friction of Scarlet's cunt as he fucked it deeply, his mind hardly able to concentrate on anything else. "My lands... aaa... my jurisdiction." He was panting. "She was a... argh... traitor!"

Half an hour must have passed by that moment. Marc was shooting a huge load into Scarlet. His cock dripped inside of her cunt as it climaxed at the same time, juices pouring out of it.

"It's not... it's not my worry now." Marc pulled out of Scarlet and lay on the ground nearby her. "She's the property of the demons at this point."

"Exactly who are the demons?" Scarlet said as she was catching her breath from Marc's rough handling.

Marc looked at the woman. "Do you really want to know?"

"They gave you that stone, didn't they?"

Marc smirked, still catching his breath as well. "Of course, they did. It's been in my family for generations."

Scarlet looked up at the sky, her eyes blank and without expression.

"My father got it from his father and so on, lines of succession. Do not think that these things come to the rich and powerful so easily."

The woman shook her head. "If all you wanted to do was... make the woman disappear... why kill those other men?"

"Blood sacrifices, dear." The man looked at Scarlet again, his eyes a little more sorrowful, more human. Scarlet wondered if it was a hint of compassion or a soul. "Do you think such beings are easy to appease?"

"All of these things are crazy... but I saw her vanish. What else could be true?"

"Many men do as I have, dear, all across the world. We recognize each other on sight. Come." The King patted the ground. "We will go back to the palace. My maids will run our baths. In the morning, we will be off to the village to make our announcement."

The two got up from the ground and dusted themselves off. Moving away from the riverbanks, the couple moved toward a horse and got on.

"Dear," Scarlet said as she sat behind her husband on the horse. "You would never do that to me, would you? Not what you did to her..."

"Stay by my side, my love, and nothing negative will ever touch you."

The two lovers rode off into the night.

As the horse galloped through the woods, a crescent moon was already shining in the darkened azure skies. Cold wind blew from the north, brushing past the couple as they moved down the winding trails lined with trees and bushes.

"It won't be too long, my love," Marc said as he held onto the steering rope connected to the horse's neck brace.

Soft wailing noises seemed to flow from between the oaks and willows. Scarlet assumed that it was merely her imagination playing with her. She wasn't afraid of the dark, but as a tribeswoman, she was use to all creatures of the night that one had to be on guard for. Wolves and bears filled many a forest, demanding respect. Along with beasts, who could forget highway robbers? Murderers?

As if I were any different, Scarlet mused without humor. The murdering acts from earlier in the night did repeat in her mind. Here she was, dreaming of getting out of the cold and having a nice hot bath to clean her skin, while a group of men laid dead. An obviously rich woman was missing, swallowed up by some void. It was a strange tunnel that appeared out of nowhere. Inky black hands pulled her into its spiraling concave madness. After she was pulled in, the portal vanished as quickly as it had appeared. It had all happened when Marc held up that stone – that strange black stone that he refused to explain to her. The whole thing frightened her.

Marc seemed so cool, relaxed, and mellow. As Scarlet clung onto him for dear life, she wondered what happened to that man that seemed to have so much soul, so warm, and so bubbly in personality. When she looked at him now, she thought she could still feel that person she met initially: even so, the looming shadow of a killer also seemed to taint those eyes. He must have done this many times. How could she ever go back to the way it was?

How could she reverse being a killer too?

The castle was visible now. It was tall with a cerulean painted exterior, its towers tall and pointy. Sentinels stood watch at the front of a big gate.

"Home, darling," Marc said as he drew closer.

As soon as the King approached, the guards bowed their heads before helping each other to pull the big door open. The horse gave a quick trot, bringing the couple inside as the heavy doors closed again. Scarlet looked around innocently at the courtyard as a few knights and ladies walked around calmly, greeting them individually as they passed by. Scarlet had been here many times over the past week, but it was taking her a while to get used to the grand sights. All the walkways were lit with candle stands on the sides and huge banners held the King's seal over every wall.

A servant obediently grabbed the horse's

reins when the King stopped in front of him. After Marc got off the horse, he helped Scarlet down, leading her inside of the palace as the servant took the horse to the stables.

"You like it here," King Marc said calmly with a smirk as Scarlet held her arm. The grip became tighter, and for a brief moment, she smiled.

As soon as the pair entered the palace, there were already handmaidens taking the King's coat and the woman's shoes. Seeing the bloody mess, they seemed completely undisturbed as they announced that they would get the bath water ready. Leaving the two alone in the hall, the maids ran upstairs as Scarlet took a look around. In the palace, even the halls were wide with a variety of paintings and sculptors against the walls and corners. The floor was shiny and there were marble columns everywhere.

A voice spoke out from behind one of the columns – it was a very deep and theatrically whimsical male voice. "I see my friend has come back from hunting. May I see the catch? "

Scarlet was a bit startled, lifting a hand to the front of her breasts as she saw the man stepping out from behind the column. He was a big man, taller than Marc, with a slightly heavy figure. His beard was full and dark, running down to the middle of his round stomach. He looked strong. His face was rugged and rough with an unsightly boil shared between his chin and left cheek. His clothes were a bit tattered and unkempt while at the same time having an eccentric and even rich appeal. Maybe he wasn't a very wealthy man, but he looked well fed and of some reasonable wealth.

Marc laughed, "Roman, how I envy your skills of surprise!"

Roman tiptoed playfully before walking a remaining two feet toward the couple, his eyes staring up and down Scarlet's form. "So, Marcus, I see you have a new angel to add to your collection. What is this, wife number 72?"

"She will be my ninth wife."

"How beautiful. Have you set a date?"

Scarlet spoke a little nervously. "No, not yet, we–"

"We will be very soon," Marc said as he stepped in front of his wife, looking directly at Roman with a smirk. "I would only give it a couple of days before this lovely woman will be an official member of the royal family."

Roman chuckled, "Oh, well that is very nice, your majesty." Looking at the bloodstains on Marc, Roman couldn't help but have a goofy smile as his arms folded, his body tilting comically. "That boar must have put up a fight, eh? Just what did you catch today?"

"You know what we catch today." Marc's response was straightforward, not cold but emotionless.

"I what?"

You know what we caught today."

"Oh." Roman reeled back from her tilting. His grin grew a bit more devious. "I see. Huh. Well, isn't that nice." Sighing, Roman's face gained some seriousness. "So, shall we discuss those affairs?"

"Allow us to wash, Roman. Afterward, I can find some entertainment for the lady while we have our conversation.

"I thought that out, Marcus. I've brought some of my friends from the circus. Allow them to entertain the lady and other members of the court while we discuss our private matters."

Marcus nodded. "Okay. That is fine. I'm placing some trust in you."

"Hopefully for you, dear friend, that will be a wise decision."

"For your sake, it would better be."

"Fine, brother, fine." Roman took a step back before turning around and walking out of the hall.

With a few loud claps, the King had summoned his handmaidens. The bathwater was ready.

Scarlet sat in the bathwater as two handmaidens slowly washed her body with well-matted rags and sponges. The soaps they used produced a fine aroma that the village girl couldn't really pinpoint but she could hardly complain. The privilege of being pampered and handled like this, Scarlet thought, could really go to a girl's head, so why not indulge?

The women were cute and seemed to be near Scarlet's age, in their 20s but a little older. They both had brown hair held in buns over the napes of their necks and wore simple peasant clothes. For working in such a fancy environment, the women were pretty common but exceptionally beautiful.

Even as the water had turned reddish pink from the blood washing off her skin, Scarlet noticed how reserved and focused the maids where. They only wanted to serve the future Queen, make her comfortable and attend to every need. She noticed how they merely looked at her skin as it glistened in the water, paying extra attention to her shiny nipples as they stood erect on her breasts.

What were Marc and that man going to talk about? Scarlet did wonder about it a few times, as the women made passing glances on her body. Were they checking her out? Their motions seemed so calm, so mechanical, but their eyes were so fixated on her skin. At times, they would look up and give her a smile that could look respectable, pleasant, but there was some sort of deviance there as well.

Scarlet arched her back. Her legs had spread a little as she did it. Maybe it was all an invitation. Scarlet really didn't know. She just knew she was really horny.

The handmaidens could sense it. Suddenly, one of the rags went down to brush the lips of her pussy. The sensation of the rag sort of tickled with its soft and fuzzy texture. Another rag from the second handmaiden continued to stroke and massage her breasts, handling her nipples playfully. Just when the tribeswoman thought her nipples couldn't get any harder, she thought they would explode in bliss.

Scarlet moaned. The moan embarrassed her; Scarlet had never been so pleasurably handled by women. Still, it felt good and she wanted to experience more. She looked at the woman as they eyed her down, the rag between her legs dipping in a bit. The woman washing her breasts dropped the rag in the water altogether, no longer able to contain herself as she opened her lips and started suckling Scarlet. Scarlet tasted so good in her mouth, the handmaiden thought.... if only she could live a day in the life of a Queen to be.

The other handmaiden looked up, still stroking Scarlet's puss with her rag, as she smiled into the mistress's eyes. Her rag also left her hand, drifting in the water as she fingered scarlet deeply. Scarlet shifted in the bathwater as she held the side of the tub, trying to compose herself, afraid of getting too loud and upsetting anyone in the castle, especially Marc. She wasn't sure where he was washing, but it would be embarrassing for him to hear how his future bride was being handled by these women. Then again, after all that she had experienced with him, she wouldn't have been surprised if he would have liked this sort of thing or even orchestrated it.

The women didn't stop. Fidgeting and digging into the woman's cunt, the first handmaiden's hand motions were getting faster and faster. She couldn't help but to take her other hand and finger herself as well, lifting her modest dress and digging in under her hidden garments.

These sexual actions must have gone on for 10 minutes before a heavy knock came at the door.

"Hurry it up," the voice of a maid ordered, "we're still waiting to dress the misses! Don't hog her."

The women cleared their throats, composing themselves as they pulled away from Scarlet's vagina and breasts. There was no talking after that. With her skin clean, they merely used some extra water to clean her hair and reasoned that they were done with her.

As much as Scarlet had enjoyed her little adventure, she was glad that it was over. She wanted to join her King and be back in his arms.

Even though the maids that dressed her flirted a bit, Scarlet was glad that they hadn't tried to make any moves on her. She already felt a little guilty about her strange lesbian fling in the bathtub. It would only make things worse to feel like she could cheat on Marc anymore. It had all happened so quickly. Her mind went back and forth on how acceptable this behavior must have been here. She was afraid of bringing up the matter with Marc – she didn't want anyone to be reprimanded or, at worst, beheaded. Maybe it was better to act as if nothing happened.

The clothes the women had dressed her in were nice – a beautiful night gown with frills. Scarlet had descended the stairs to look for Marc. She could hear his voice and the voice of his comrade at a pretty high volume. She wondered what they were talking about and cared to listen. At first, it seemed like talk to just catch up. The closer she got, however, the tone of the conversation seemed very serious.

Scarlet could tell that they were in one of the meeting rooms that the King had pointed out to her before. She approached slowly, not wanting to disturb them.

"And you've handled the stone well, my brother?" Roman asked quite audibly.

"The stone takes care of you," Marc responded. "And you know that."

The stone. They were talking about that weird stone Scarlet saw. The stone that made that woman vanish. Scarlet knew that. She had to approach coolly, slowly. Then she stopped. Just listen, she thought, listen.

After some silence, Scarlet heard Marc speak again. "I don't know if I can do it, brother. Keep appeasing these demons. Allow their want for blood to ruin my life. I know they gave my family everything – this castle, this kingdom – but the things they demand, money. Sex, and death, it's evil! They have reduced the subjects of my castle into sex fiends. They've brought shame to our culture for three hundred years. And now they want me to conquer these tribes people, to unite the kingdom and introduce an age of debauchery!"

"Well, imagine how I feel brother," Roman said, interrupting. "All day I go about, in every town I visit, looking for new playthings for the demons. Why the last woman I used was one of my staff! She was an excellent performer. How do you think I felt?"

"Well... my sympathies go to you, brother," Marc said in a sorrowful voice that Scarlet found believable. "I just wish I could relate to your situation more. I run a kingdom, and I respect your talents and our shared family burdens, but... I don't think I can do what the demons are demanding of me, now."

"You must," Roman said. "You must do all that they ask."

A hand fell onto Scarlet's shoulder. The men continued to talk in the room, but their words lost Scarlet's focus as she now looked to the woman behind her. It was another maid, smiling calmly. "Come see the circus acts that Roman kindly provided, miss."

The maid led the woman out of the room. Scarlet looked over her shoulder once and then let it all go. What was she doing? Playing with women, eavesdropping, she had to get it together. She would continue the night in a clean and respectable manner.

Scarlet did enjoy the show – a male and a female very skilled in fire breathing, juggling, and other tricks kept her entertained while her future husband met with his guest.

When the show was done, Scarlet greeted her King in the hall. Roman had already headed to his room for bed.

"What did you two talk about?"

Marc sighed as he carried Scarlet up the stairs. "We were catching up. Roman is an old friend of mine. He's a ringmaster from a circus. My father employed him years ago, and he traveled through the kingdom. Now, he does pretty well for himself and does shows in many countries. The business is his own now, but we still talk from time to time."

"Is he of royal descent? It seemed like he spoke so casually with you."

"We have history."

It was silent for a while as Marc stopped in front of his bedchamber, still holding the future Queen in his arms.

"Marc," Scarlet said as she rubbed a hand on the King's neck, "when am I going to meet your other wives?"

"I keep them all in separate parts of the castle, my dear. I've explained this to you before. They are very jealous."

"I just don't feel comfortable sometimes... thinking of all these secrets you keep from me. After today – "

"We need to take our time. The more that you become a part of the royal family, the more you will know. Now, dear, can we please make love?" Marc leaned in and kissed his wife softly, flickering a little of his tongue against hers.

"Well," Scarlet said with a smile, "fine then. I'm ready."

Marc slowly opened the door, pushing it open with his left foot as the doors opened wide. Scarlet pressed against Marc's chest as she caught a sight of the big bed, but it took her a while to trust her eyes and what she was seeing on top of it. Over the fluffy pillows and thick blankets sat two very attractive brown-haired women in the nude. They were the handmaidens from the bath earlier.

"Marc," Scarlet said with a shock that robbed any emotion.

"Scarlet, I'm sure you have met my lovely maids earlier, during your bath. They will be accompanying us for our love session."

Scarlet felt her senses slowly returning, her head shaking as she got out of Marc's arms and looked up at him. "Marc, this isn't –"

"Scarlet, please don't disrespect our guests." Marc closed the door behind him as he took Scarlet by the hand and pulled her toward the waiting females. "They got a little taste this evening but I promised them a full meal."

The woman slowly moved from the bed with seductive walks as their expressions looked so enticed with Scarlet.

Scarlet reached her hands up to Marc. "Marc, I've done many things for you, and I would do anything, but we need privacy."

One of the handmaidens ripped the back of Scarlet's nightgown. Scarlet shrieked a bit before gaining control of herself, watching as the women reached from her now exposed breasts and licked them together. Cupping them in their hands, they closed their eyes and suckled the nipples delicately. Though Scarlet protested at first, it wasn't long before she was arching her back, leaning into the women. They escorted her to the bed as Marc reached for a chair and pulled it toward him, taking a seat. "I'll watch!"

Scarlet nearly protested this request but the handling of her breasts felt so good. A slender hand had already worked its way up into her cunt. It was too nice, the way it felt, and until this day she never thought that she could derive any sensual treatment from another woman, let alone two. They must have been pros. Scarlet laid on her back as they rubbed against her thighs and arms, one of them finding their way to her cunt and eating her out. The forced pushing of the tongue in her cunt just made her feel so good, the circular motions so fast and akin to a hurricane.

"Treat her politely, girls. I know you've wanted this."

"Mm hmm." The one still playing with her nipples said before looking into Scarlet's eyes with a smile. Her eyes were so beautiful and deep, complex with movement. At one moment, Scarlet saw them shine in the light and mused on how they were quite unique in comparison to any set of eyes she had seen before. For such modest servants, these women pleased Scarlet's sight without complaints.

"Oooh..." Scarlet said as the handmaiden between her legs seemed to be hitting so many pleasurable points. The tongue dipped in and out with a slippery movement, and although Scarlet loved Marc's cock, this tongue was equally as fun. Scarlet felt bad for not returning the favor, and at one point, she tried to lift off her back to return the favors the women were giving her. There wasn't really a chance; they had her pinned down, tongues travelling inside and outside of her. Scarlet decided it was best to leave it this way. Why ruin a good thing?

When she was able to lift her head a bit, she could see Marc beating himself off with his pants to his ankles.

The woman between her legs continued to lick deeply, her fingers slipping inside of Scarlet's ass and fingering her playfully. Scarlet thought it was weird that she would slip her fingers up there – she had never had anyone play with her ass in such a way. It was a bit embarrassing to her, but every time she thought about how weird it was, she would feel the pleasure that came with it. In a moment's time, she was pushing her asshole against the fingers with as much intensity as she was pushing her cunt into the mouth.

"Oh god, please don't stop!" Scarlet said. She didn't know how much time had passed – it felt like she had been getting eaten out for minutes now. "Keep it... keep it up. I'm sure I'll blow soon!"

"Mmmm," the woman said between her legs as she continued to eat her out mercilessly.

"My sister likes your pussy, miss," the maid near the breasts said as she lifted up from the nipples to look Scarlet in the eyes and kiss her softly.

When the kiss ended and the maid pulled her lips away, Scarlet looked at her dreamingly. "Well yes, it would seem so. Ooooo.... you're... sisters?

"Oh, we're all sisters here," the woman said before bending back down and kissing the woman all over her breasts.

Marc watched with intensity. He had seen many a session like this but it never got old.

"Ohhh..." Scarlet said with a swing of the head.

"Dear," Marc said as he felt his cock throbbing in excitement between his right hand. "I'm so glad that you could meet two of my beautiful guests. You see, Denise there," he said, pointing to the woman between Scarlet's legs with his left hand, "is an excellent lover. Very satisfactory. Tasha, as you can understand, is a little new to this, but she's been doing pretty well."

"Mmmm," Scarlet said as she felt the women handling her body like a toy. Before long, she had noticed how far the tongue was inside of her. It was pretty fair; she was surprised it could reach like this. It was almost like an extendable dick.

Suddenly, Scarlet's moans were replaced with a swallowing gag. She tried to regain her breathe as she realized this tongue – this strange tongue – was very deep inside of her, inhumanly deep. Could it have even passed the limit of her vagina? She could hardly think or rationalize what was going on. All she could feel was that this thing growing inside of her seemed to travel higher and higher through her body, spreading in an almost fluid motion. What she had mistaken for a woman tongue now felt like a dripping, sliding mess that was both liquid and solid. It gave pain and pleasure at the same time, but more than anything, it brought an extreme feeling of violation.

As the strange woman between her legs, Denise, continued to push this awful splattering mess into her, black liquid dripped on the blankets from her chin. Tasha could feel her eyes blacking out as she felt black liquid dripping down on her breasts. It was covering her like the blood covered her from earlier, memories of a portal and black inky hands coming back to her.

These were those mystery beings. They had to be.

"Don't be so afraid," Marc said as cum sputtered out of his cock. "They just want to make love to you." His hand reached into his pocket after his selfish orgasm was over. He pulled out the black stone, its surface dark and shiny. It instantly started to glow.

A figure stepped from out of the closet. It was Roman, adjusting his pants and looking at the woman handling their craft. Both men had seen it all before – the protesting shakes and jolts from the conquered damsel, the transformation of the human female disguises into their demonic inky forms, and the dripping of black substance and residue on the blankets. There was no need to worry; all of the mess would clean itself up at the end of the session, going back into the world that the stones connected to.

What was once Scarlet was now a dripping dark form, still protesting and kicking, as the otherworldly women held her in their grip.

"Sacrifices," Marc said calmly without shame as he stood up, holding the stone and coming closer to the bed. "That is what is needed to gain anything, Scarlet. Sacrifices. My family worked too hard for all of this. Now, I must continue to do my work."

One of the dark beings sneered and cackled. "We need sex and we need blood."

"You will understand, dear," the other demon said.

"They all understand, sooner or later, Scarlet," Marc said as he laughed. "Believe me, it's better this way. I only allow the women I love to be initiated. I couldn't have let you go out as a blood sacrifice, not like that."

The demons laughed.

"Goodbye, my love."

Finally, a portal opened over the bed. It was dark and hallow, a dirty stench blowing from it. More hands reached out from it, taking Scarlet as the dark women handed her to them. After ensuring that she had gone in completely, the demons followed her, leaping up into the circle and vanishing in the night.

The two men stood frozen, watching the room calm down to normal. The blankets were ruffled, the air of the room filled with sex, and the rancid smell that demons brought. There was not a black stain waiting to be clean.

Roman looked at Marc. "Tasha has learned well in over a month. I must say that I am proud of her."

Marc chuckled as he looked to the floor before staring back at his comrade. "She's doing pretty well, I would say."

"So what do you plan now?"

"Well," Marc said before taking a big breath, "I'll do as I usually do. Send a few platoons out. Wipe out her entire village. Kill them all."

"That helps you suppress a threat?"

"It may help you to indoctrinate naïve whores from your circus and audiences. The art of courtship suits me fine, if you ask me."

"As you wish, your majesty," Roman replied mockingly. Walking up to the bed, he bent his head down and sniffed the blankets. A smile grew wide as he lifted back up. "Well. In the morning, I will be off and on the lookout for more places to perform. It's hard maintaining this work but how can I complain? I live to entertain. I can only thank the demons for making my circus so successful. Thank the demons."

"Thank the demons."

Roman turned and started to walk toward the door. Stopping before he even touched the doorknob, he looked toward Marc with sincerity. "I count on you as a brother in service to the demonic stones, brother. I won't forget our conference with the others. "

"Three months, brother. Don't miss it."

With a final nod, Roman opened the door and left the King behind in his empty bedroom. Marc was never too worried to sleep alone – he was convinced that there would always be a new maiden to bring into his chambers. The world held many pleasures. He couldn't blame the demons for indulging – they needed their drink of blood and sex. All that he asked was that, with the wealth and prestige they had given him, they would allow him to do the same.

2 ABYSS OF THE DEMONS 2
DEMON CIRCUS

The circus was coming to town. It was a special circus with a very strict rule—adults only.

The circus was the most famous one in the world. It had been run for centuries, traveling from country to country and entertaining large audiences with impressive feats and acts. There were lion tamers, strippers, clowns, acrobats, actors, and ringleaders. That wasn't all the circus brought to town. Elephants performed tricks, freaks with different birth defects stood in booths for anyone that wished to see them, and drifters set up tents and worked for a hot meal. The circus survived through the people, remaining a community affair, and it would always stay that way.

The owner of the circus was still grieving from the death of his father. The father was a man that had always seemed so happy and cheery. Surprisingly, he committed suicide, devastating the church in his passing. His will had already been worked out with everything the father owned now in the possession of his son. Still, the son was convinced that he could take the mantle of the circus by the horns successfully without a problem. The father left him a large amount of cash after his death. The son couldn't be too upset with the inheritance he had gained. Still, he wasn't a greedy person, and he loved his father. He was just glad that he didn't have to starve. With a circus, a loyal family, tons of wealth, and some strange, exotic looking stones his father gave him, he was sure he'd make his way in the world.

As Christopher, the new ringleader and owner of The Dreaming Circus, laid on his bed and allowed his wife to ride him like a horse trainer, he smiled. He held his wife's hips and stared up at her bouncing tits, her red hair teasing her shoulders so playfully as it curled and whipped up and down repeatedly. God, she was beautiful. He had always thought that about her. From her tanned skin to her lengthy legs and pleasing physique, he had instantly fallen in love with her. This was the person he wanted to be with for the rest of his life. If anything happened, Christopher would do anything for her.

The woman's name was Jessica. Before she had joined the circus, she had been a mere prostitute, roaming the streets of some god-forsaken town riddled with plague and disease. How she got out of the place young, vibrant, and healthy with an unmatchable beauty, Chris didn't know. They were both in the prime of their lives, only a few years into adulthood and owning a circus dynasty. Christ hoped that he wouldn't be frivolous or lured by pretty sights like his father. He had set to stay with Jessica and Jessica would be it. No other woman would break up the love that they had together.

"Oh, Chris!" Jessica said as she whined, her eyes closed with her hands grabbing at her husband's chest. "I think I'm going to... I'm going to..."

"Do it baby," Chris said as he grabbed his wife's ass and made her ride harder. "Whatever you're going to do, do it."

Chris was teasing her, of course. He knew that the only thing she was ready to do was climax. He felt her do it too. When his cock pressed in a few final times, he felt her squirting like an oil leak as Jessica screamed to high heaven. Thank god everyone else was asleep, unless they woke them up!

It was the dead of night. The circus tents were all packed up, and the wagons had already hit the dirt roads. Whatever country they were going to, they weren't really sure. It didn't matter much to Christopher though. He knew that wherever they went, he was sure to get a crowd or audience. The only thing Chris didn't much like about traveling were the politics between countries. Sometimes it was truly hard to know if there was any drama going on in a kingdom. There might have been a war or a conflict. Then Chris's wagons would either have to take some back roads or produce papers to cross borders and stay on the good sides of soldiers and kings. Chris hated having to play into the hands of the rich and spoiled royals like that, but being a person that considered himself a citizen of the world required respecting the laws of the world, no matter where his circus roamed.

"Your father would be proud of you, Christopher," Jessica said with a smile. "You're a regular Casanova, just like him."

"Oh, stop," Christopher said with a grin. "I'm hardly anything like my father. Don't get me wrong, I loved the man, but I can even say that he was a bit of a selfish asshole."

"I bet he had a soft side at times, Christopher." Jessica smiled. "You shouldn't be so hard on people. He did all that he could, didn't he?"

"I guess that can be said. Even so, I don't know." Christopher sighed. "I have always thought the man to be a bit vain, womanizing, and stern. That's why I had always been so adamant on having a normal relationship—not just fucking carnies and sideshow whores. Then I met you."

"But Chris, you know that I used to be a whore. I was immersed into that whole lifestyle."

"You're different, Jess. Believe me. When I look into your eyes, I know that you are real."

Jessica blushed. "You're so sweet."

As Jessica lifted up from Christopher's lap, she teased her red hair and walked over to the dresser. She removed the earrings she was wearing and hummed a pretty little tune to herself. No sooner had she walked up to the dresser had she found something that caught her eyes like Medusa. She picked up a pretty black stone. "Christopher, you have a lot of these and I've seen them before, but what are they?"

Christopher laughed. "An inheritance from my father. Apparently he loved stones." Christopher shrugged. "I don't get it. He said they had been passed down from family member to family member. They're interesting, though. Personally, I love them, just the shiny black exterior. I often wonder where they came from originally."

Jessica shrugged as she put the stone down. "A pretty stone, nonetheless." Walking over to her husband, she trailed some fingers on his chest before kissing him. "We should go to bed now. We're going to have quite a busy day in the morning, don't you think?"

"It won't be too bad. I just have to patrol the grounds, make sure everyone sets up appropriately. Check on the different acts and make sure that everyone is preparing for their roles in the next circus show."

"And me?"

Christopher leaned in and grinned. "You'll be practicing your horseback riding, jumping from horse to horse and doing all sorts of tricks on them."

Jessica smiled. "That's nice, dear. I love to be your professional horse trainer and rider, but you know there's only one real horse I like to ride, one that is a pleasure to work on."

Jessica grabbed Christopher's dick as it hung out for the bedroom. Instantly, Christopher became hard again.

"You just want a round two," Christopher said with a tease.

"We have a busy day tomorrow, but... sex is pretty rejuvenating, don't you think?"

"Baby... after fucking you, three hours of sleep seems enough."

The two were back at it again. There would be time to catch up on rest later.

The circus grounds were getting set up. After the wagons had found a close enough town to entertain, they stopped. Hauling out equipment and setting up tents, the carnies and temporary drifters that wandered nearby got to work, knowing the pay later would be satisfactory.

"Get to work!" Christopher screamed to the carnies as he saw them wake up. He was nice often and fair, but when it came to a job, Christopher knew how to crack the whip.

People rarely took it too harshly, especially Christopher's workers. They all got on their game, picking up materials and rushing to put things up.

As the workers set up the stands and tents, performers got outside and practiced their little tricks. Clowns out of costume and makeup practiced their juggling, fire dancers danced with unlit sticks, and acrobats did some flips and spins on the trampoline. Everyone was making sure they had their routines down so that they could be safe, avoiding their own injury and the injury of their coworkers and audiences. All of this was very important in the line of circus working.

Jess was already taking the horses out and practicing her routine. Christopher never got bored with watching her. Through the act she continued to hop from horse to horse as one of the clowns practiced chasing after her like a love-enflamed stalker, unable to catch up with the circle of horses that loyally followed the course they were trained for.

Smiling, Christopher placed a hand on his cheek as he admired his wife's beauty.

"You were lucky to land that one," a voice said from behind Christopher.

Christopher turned around to see Antoine, one of the principal fire breathers. In all respects, Christopher never liked Antoine. Ever since he joined the circus, Antoine made it his main priority to tell everyone just how close he and Christopher's father had been. He was always so proud, bragging about how many circus women he had fucked with Chris's father, audience women and random ladies in their walks on the town. The bearded, wild-eyed, and tall potbelly of a freak seemed to think constantly of nothing other than sex with strange women. Such company in his circus truly made Christopher nervous.

"I would prefer if you didn't eye hound my wife, Antoine."

Antoine's eyes opened widely with amusement as he lifted his hands in a truce. "Oh, pardon me, sir. I was merely commenting with how pretty she looked."

"From your many stories, I am well aware of how that usually ends up, sir." Chris frowned as he turned back to look at the horses.

"Okay, okay, I'm sorry. Damn!" The man looked out to the field with the ringmaster, still admiring the woman that Christopher had claimed as his own. "Say there, why are you in such a bitter mood?"

Christopher growled. "Well, for one thing, Antoine, as you are well aware of, I don't like you. I hate your guts and I think you are deplorable as a human being. As a second thing, well, I would rather just watch my wife in peace."

"Have you played with the stones yet?"

Christopher felt stunned for a reason. It took a while for him to gather in his mind that he had never talked to Antoine about the stones that he had gathered from his father nor did he know that Antoine would know anything about them. Turning to the bearded rogue, Christopher eyed the man with a sense of suspicion. "Why do you ask?"

Antoine shook his head. "Fuck! Can't talk about anything with your whiny, spoiled ass getting your panties all scrunched up. Okay, listen. Me and your father had fun with those stones, quite a few times on our escapades."

Christopher laughed. "Oh? What did you do? Shine them up nice and pretty so that girls would come flocking for miles?"

Antoine smirked. "Didn't have to shine them. They stay pretty smooth all on their own. And the stones didn't help us get girls. We had to do all the work. The stones, on the other hand…"

As Antoine trailed off, Christopher reasoned that the man was just toying with him for some reason. What the hell would be so interesting with a couple of stones? Everything really angered Christopher.

"All I really have to say, Chris," Antoine said before yawning and starting to walk away, "is that soon, an audience has to pay their pipers. Just like an audience would have to pay a booth master at a circus. You, my friend, are an audience."

Chris sighed. He was used to hearing Antoine trail off into egotistical riddle banter. Sometimes, he swore that Antoine was more of a clown than the clowns were. "Will you just fuck off, Antoine!?"

"My pleasure, majesty of the circus." Antoine grinned before frowning. Turning around, he walked away, leaving Christopher to contemplate the mysterious nature of stones.

"Come on, Chris, we can afford to have another sex session!"

Chris was fucking Jess once more in their bedroom. This time they were standing upright. Jess was pressed against the dresser, sweating like crazy. Her ass was out, granted to Chris as he fucked her from behind. Chris continued to finger and fist her as hard as he could. Sometimes, it surprised him by how much Jess could take into her cunt. Weren't women built with as much of a limit as anything else? Sometimes, the energy of Jess seemed unyielding. She would just stand up, thrusting her ass back as Chris slammed his cock in, allowing him to work his cock into her. He wanted the feeling to last, but he had a circus to run!

There she was, her hands perfectly positioned, her skin dripping sweat. She even dripped a great deal of sweat on the stones as they sat on the dresser. It made Chris laugh, remembering his conversation with Antoine earlier in the day. Paying pipers. What a tool.

"Ahh...aaaaaa... ahhhh!" Chris was surprised that Jess had held her composure without screaming this time. It was he that was shouting now, climaxing into her ass and feeling his cock shot a silver, wet spray of cum into her. God! She was so pretty, so smooth in his hands, so...

"I love you," Jess said as she turned around to kiss her husband.

"And I love you, too."

The two kissed each other deeply, passionately. Chris thought about his father. The ringleader also thought about how he had to grow up without a mother, seeing whore-to-whore make their way into the house. That wasn't the life he wanted. He had his own woman, and maybe one day, when they could leave the circus, they could form their own family. There was no way Christopher was going to run a circus with kids around, growing up the way he did. No way!

Suddenly, Jess jerked her head up with bulging eyes, moaning.

Christopher was flabbergasted at first, wondering if Jess was really having an orgasm right then and there, after their sex session. He would soon learn that was not the case. Instead, Jess was having some strange insertion slamming into her asshole. It was black, amorphous, and nearly liquidly, dripping on the floor and extending from one of the stones on the dresser.

"What the fuck?" Christopher thought as she saw the weird thing moving from the stone and inside of his wife. It was the exact same color as the stone, just as smooth, and it was entering his life in her ass like a dick. Still, Christopher could tell it was going in way too deeply and unnaturally.

"Get the fuck out of her!" Chris screamed frantically as he tried to pull out the thing. Suddenly, the thing burned his hand. Chris leaped back with a yell as his wife cried, the blackness entering her quickly. Soon black ooze spewed out of her mouth and her eyes. Her legs shivered and kicked as she lay on the floor, suffering from spasms. Black ooze was pouring out of every crevice—her mouth, eyes, nose, ears, pussy, ass...

"Get out of her!" Christopher said as he grabbed his hair wildly, losing his mind. "What's wrong with you?"

Looking to his side, Chris saw one of his swords he had gathered from his circus travels. It was a gift from an accommodating king. Grabbing it quickly, Chris rushed toward the black thing to cut its extension from the stone.

It was too late. The thing had already entered his wife completely.

Jess's skin was turning a slithery, silvery, and shiny black. Her features were disappearing behind a humanoid mask of her former self. She was covered with a symbiotic mess now, and soon she was helping herself up, standing upright as she rubbed her sides and her stomach. She took a while to gain some composure, some strength, before a laugh exited her lips.

Christopher was not fully convinced that the laugh was completely Jess's.

The dripping of the black had stopped. It became smooth and as solid as a rock. Her hair was completely out of sight, her eyes unseen. Christopher could make a bit of a shape of a nose and the bridging of eyebrows, a soft outlining of lips. There were some things that still made the woman seem human or real. Still, Chris couldn't be completely sure that she was human. He was afraid that there would be even more changes that he would have to witness and endure. At this point and time, he couldn't run or give up on trying to free her from whatever happened. He loved her, and he would try to look for a way to reverse all of this.

Staring at Christopher, the black thing mused as it looked at the husband's sword. "So are you going to kill me with that thing now?"

Christopher dropped the sword in fear and shock. "What the hell do you want and why are you here?"

"You are indebted to us, human." The black thing stepped forward a bit, some strange screeching coming from its stomach. "Family debts upon family debts."

Christopher looked down at the thing's stomach. "What is that noise?"

A screeching sounded again.

"Jess," the thing answered simply. "Being transformed forever."

Christopher picked up his sword and shouted loudly. "Then I'm going to split you open!"

"And open the floodway to the abyss?"

Christopher was confused, puzzled. He stumbled back. "What the fuck... abyss?"

"The void. Death. Hell to the wicked, heaven to the lovely. All in all, it's the same thing, isn't it? What do you think?"

"I think you're a fucking bastard and that I'm going to kill you!"

The black thing shook its head. "You will do no such thing. In fact, we will tell you what to do." Suddenly, the thing's voice was sounding like a choir of voices—an evil, ungodly choir with subdued melodies. "You will enter back into that human world you live, the pathetic one. You will find us women on which to feed. You will grant us entryway to their vaginas, assholes, and mouths. Then we will be survived and our legion will grow and grow."

Christopher shook his head, starting to cry. "Why? Why do I have to do this?"

"Because you signed the agreements for your father's will. You accepted his gifts."

The tears rolled down Christopher's cheek in anguish. "You really want me to just sign my life away to you freaks?"

"You already did."

"Fuck! Where is Jess?"

"Jess is one of us now. We are legion and we are many."

"You're fucking evil... that's what you are!"

"Soon you will be evil, too." The thing seemed to grin from its outlined lips. "Now, human, you will feed our abyss. You will only share our secret to the worthy. Your blood is bound to the pact."

"And if I refuse?"

"You won't, and you cannot."

Somehow, in a strange way, Christopher felt like the thing was right. Even in trying to think contrary to what the thing wanted him to do, Christopher was at a lost for thought.

"Now you must go into the world and find

us more victims. More women. More pleasures!"

That night started it all. Jess became a distant memory; someone that Christopher said ran away and wanted to go back to whoring. She just couldn't cut it in the marriage life, he said. It didn't fulfill her like what she was born to do.

The show that night had been successful. The circus was able to move on to another country by the time that seven women were reported missing in that area.

Christopher proved to be quite the successful ringmaster. He was good at enticing women, flirting with them, and bonding with them. At many times, they would come to visit him in his little wagon. Very rarely if ever did any of the circus performers see the women exit the wagon. No one asked questions, however. Like father, like son.

Even Antoine, the rogue that had been a fly in Antoine's mouth, became a dear and entrusted friend. They shared their escapades together, sometimes swapping women before the ladies would disappear altogether. Christopher was sure that his relationship with Antoine had become an amicable one when he saw the stones Antoine owned himself.

"As you see, Christopher," Antoine said with a firm look, patting the ringmaster on the back. "We all start out good, I'm sure. But who knows what destiny has in the fates of men? Who knows what the stars really say?"

"I'm not an astrologer," Christopher responded. "Just a simple circus performer."

Performing was something they had to do to survive—going from country to country and fucking a feast of women. After five years of travel, Christopher had seen many naked breast sizes and had felt so many different textures and wet sensations from woman all over the world. He had given his all to the sex act, pleasing and romancing women to climax as he fucked them doggy style, missionary, and orally. Some of the women even let him do really kinky things, like shove his foot inside of them or tie them up and fuck them from behind. No matter how they explored their pleasures, they would all end up the same way. The stones would smell their scent or feel their sweat, and open up. The women would be dragged into the dimension of the abyss or transformed right then and there in the human world. From there, the legion had more lovers in their ranks. Women of a variety of sizes, shapes, and colors served them well.

"You know," one of the female demons said as it appeared to Christopher while he slept, "you are a good fucker."

Christopher woke up with a start before frowning. "You reason so?"

The demon mused with a chuckle and grin. "We've watched you many times."

Christopher frowned as he turned around, trying to get some sleep.

The demon trailed a finger on the human's chest. "You know, we don't just convert women. We convert men, too."

A shiver moved down Christopher's spine.

"We just wanted you to get women because we knew that was what you would be comfortable with... and what you would be good at."

Christopher frowned as he turned around to look at the demon. "Fuck you! You want me to gather men now?"

"Not exactly."

"Good. Because I'm not a–"

The demon pressed a strong finger against Christopher's mouth, silencing him instantly. "Shhh," the demon said. "You speak far too much. Listen, Christopher. We've been with your family for a long time—centuries. You've all done us proud and we've made a decision. It ends tonight."

"Tonight?"

"Yes, tonight. The family debt. You've all suffered long enough."

Christopher shook his head. "And why, suddenly, after leeching off my family for so long, making us do evil things... and turning us evil, would you want it to end?"

"Because you will be the perfect sacrifice."

Before Christopher could protest, the strong female demon was grabbing Christopher close with its shiny black fingers. It took its mouth and pressed against Christopher, tonguing him deeply. Christopher wanted to scream, but a strong black ooze completely filled his mouth, shoving itself down his throat. Christopher started to cry black rivers of sadness, his body feeling as if it was in an acidic fire. He felt like he was melting from the interior, melding with this demon as it had its way with him. He was merely a tool for it to exert its strange sexual desires on, and soon he was going to the abyss.

A figure entered the room. Christopher looked up to see a grinning Antoine.

"No need for your family to suffer, Chrissy boy." Antoine grinned evilly. "I'll be taking your stones, there. I know many kings that would love for me to sell them."

With the ability to scream gone, Christopher blacked out, completely surrounded by a dark, black void.

4 VINEYARDS AND GARDENS

The sun was shining throughout a long range of mountains patched with rocky sides, green fields, and a variety of forests. It was daybreak. The smell of spring was everywhere. From blossoming flowers to the sweet smells of herbs lining the country roads, beauty surrounded this paradise. Some men and women were already in the gardens, gathering vegetables and fruit, squashing grapes for wine. The mountain life required a rigor and strong work ethic, which many outsiders did not understand if they hadn't been raised in the country. Still, even with the hard work, there was a sense of being connected to nature that was more felt than thought. Everyone who lived here accepted their role in working and maintaining a balance for their community.

This was just the human community. Close to their seemingly insulated world, there existed another community. Very few were privileged enough to find it.

"These mountains," a husband said to his wife as she picked through grapes by his side, "are the property of Dionysus, the lord of our vineyards and gardens. To him, we must give praise every day of our lives."

The wife was new to these mountains. Her name was Aglaia, a woman from Athens. "We worshiped him well in my city," Aglaia responded, "but it's nice to be in his humble abode. I've dreamed of this for years."

Her husband, Agrios, smiled as he dropped another bundle of grapes into his basket. "You will love it here. It is by the grace of Dionysus that we found each other."

The wife pointed toward one of the long winding paths that seemed to be far off in the distance. "The past few weeks I've been here, I've heard some strange noises going on over there. They're like panpipes and flutes. It's awkward sounding, lacking rhythm and structure, and yet...it's so alluring. It's usually at nighttime."

Agrios looked toward the path, his face losing its jolly appeal. He was afraid that, eventually, this would happen- but he didn't expect it so soon. "Yes. There are many things that go on down there."

Aglaia looked at her husband calmly. "Like what, may I ask?"

Agrios shook his head. "It is a mystery of Dionysus. Only the women can hear the strange sounds that come from that path at night. I've never seen one who walked that way return."

Aglaia nodded and started gathering more grapes, feeling ashamed after seeing how much the question had affected her husband. "I see. I am sorry. I didn't mean to upset you."

"Don't worry about me dear. You were curious. Believe me, I understand." The husband grabbed his wife suddenly, not roughly but abruptly, and looked her in the eye. "But I beg of you, Aglaia. Please do not follow the sounds. They may get intense, heavy even. But it is wise for a woman of your beauty and stature to ignore these sounds."

Aglaia was ready to drop the subject, but she couldn't deny her curiosity. She hoped that she wouldn't anger or upset her husband any further. "Dear, what do these sounds mean? Is someone playing music out there?"

"The voice of nature calls you," Agrios said solemnly. "Believe me, Aglaia, these lands are holy and there are many beautiful things here—but there are some things that human folk should not dwell in. The music you hear is not the music of humans. It is the music of the beings watched under the veil of our lord that owns these lands. Their ways are mysterious and strange. It is best not to entertain them." With that, Agrios picked up the basket of grapes. "Come now—I'm sure the others have gathered their own crops and are ready to make use of this harvest." With that, Agrios walked back toward the farms from which they came.

Aglaia, trying her best to be a worthy and helpful wife, followed Agrios back without any more questions. As the couple walked, they didn't see the stubby little hand of a satyr pushing back some bushes to get a good glimpse of Aglaia.

In the mountains, beyond the eyes of the human population, all sorts of activity happened, especially in the spring. Although a human could see the blossoming flowers, the green grass and fields yielding fruit all over the luscious environment, only a few could understand what was really going on. This was the season of sex, and sex was in the air, so strong and wild that it could bewilder the senses of one that got too close or connected to nature without wisdom.

It was these types that Dionysus drew his strongest bond with the ones that could appreciate the powerful senses of madness. The limber man sat calmly on his unkempt throne of grass, weeds, and rocks stained with wine. He moved a hand through his curly hair as he stared out into the field surrounding him. Countless satyrs and nymphs were spreading their sexual juices in the ground, allowing spring to spread through the soil. Many of the nymphs, beautiful with long hair flowing onto the ground, moaned and screamed as they spread their legs and opened themselves for the satyrs . The satyrs, horny little devils with goat legs and heavy horns, claimed their prizes as they slid over the women with bellies full of wine. Dionysus was truly happy for the sights, but for the past week, he was secretly dealing with a calamity that made the sights of sex less enjoyable.

One of the nymphs suddenly leaped into Dionysus's lap, laughing as she provided two breasts for his mouth. Dionysus began to suck on them willingly, enjoying their full circumference and soft texture. The nipples hardened in his mouth quickly.

"Why," the nymph said as she started to finger herself, "do you worry yourself so about these frivolous human girls?"

Dionysus looked the woman into her eyes. Sighing, he pulled out his rock-hard cock as his hand offered the woman to mount it. She willingly accepted.

"You like the chase," the nymph said with a tease. "The endless want to bring a woman to her knees, to see the divine and taste the sexual pleasures of nature."

Dionysus's face remained immobile to satisfaction.

"My nymph, you are correct."

The nymph leaned onto Dionysus as she nibbled his ear and kissed his neck.

"Aren't you tired of stealing the women of human males?"

Dionysus shook his head, ignoring the woman's question as she continued to ride his dick, her pussy wet and firm. This would have to do for now, he thought, as he supported her, letting her dip back. "I do not understand. When I call, is not a woman compelled to answer?"

"You have become arrogant in your sexual desires, dear Dionysus," the nymph said as she continued to ride the cock, her ass sticking out over Dionysus's legs. "You do not deserve to be so callous, young lord. In comparison to the other gods, do not forget your inexperience."

Dionysus held the woman as he shoved her tits in his face, continuing to suckle, pull, and tease her nipples. Keeping her rhythm steady, he started to talk again. "I travelled through the mountains and fields of Africa, sailed the oceans and seas, and hiked through the wilderness of the Asia Minor. How am I less of a god than any Olympian or any other deity? In these mountains, I am worshipped, respected, and feared. So why would any human resist me when I call?"

"Perhaps they are just nervous, my lord. You must understand—when a new one comes here—it is strange and confusing to hear such godly noises. Give it time. Soon, their want for knowledge will overwhelm them."

As clear and wordy as their conversation had been, it was a conversation of breaks, moans, groans, and heavy breaths. It was clear that Dionysus had a lot to get off of his mind—he rarely talked during sex. Still, the nymph wished he would just shut up and fuck her. She knew in her heart, however, that she was not on his list of priorities for the week.

"They always....come," the nymph said

before suddenly screaming in orgasm, pouring a huge splash of juices over Dionysus that dripped like wine.

"Yes," Dionysus said with certainty, not even cumming as he pulled out of the nymph coldly. "They do."

Collapsing after their orgy, two couples of satyrs and nymphs lay lazily as they waited to regain strength for another round.

"Do you think," one of the satyrs said, as he looked up to the skies, "that the humans will ever regain the respect for our lord that they used to?"

One of the nymphs gave a heavy breathe of annoyance. "The humans have become so weak in these later times, haven't they? All those laws and talk about modesty. I doubt those golden days will come back again."

"There was a time," one of the satyrs said with a delightful gaze in his eyes, "where these mountains ran with desire and dripped with blood."

"The days of the maenads—that was a good time," the second nymph said.

"Sex, wine, and violence," the happy satyr mused. "Freedom."

"Do not expect those days to come back again," an interrupting voice said.

They knew the voice well. The couples looked up at their lord, Dionysus, standing over them. He was still looking down, more so than they were used to seeing him.

"Are you still trying to get the human woman to join us, lord?" said one of the satyrs.

"She resists me," Dionysus answered. "I

do not know if she knows how to respond to my call. Perhaps I should give up."

"Perhaps you should keep trying," one of the nymphs said as she crawled on the ground and kissed the lord's feet. "These humans do not know how to respond to divinity at first—but in time they listen and learn. They are such frightful and reserved creatures. You know that."

Dionysus reached for his wine gourd and guzzled a bit of it. "I remember a time when I could just snap my fingers and have a row of mountain girls run toward me. This woman, she does not smell of the country."

"She is a city girl, lord."

Dionysus turned around to see another satyr behind him, out of breathe with his hands on his knees. He could tell the little guy had just run back from the path leading to the human settlement. "From Athens. She knows nothing of this natural world."

"Is she now?" Dionysus's face suddenly turned bright and amused for the first time in a while. "I see. I am well loved there. Still, no city compares to my true environment."

"She spoke about what she was hearing with her husband. I saw the curiosity in her eyes. You must call her again, Dionysus. Tonight. Then, you will have your wish and the human will be yours."

Dionysus nodded. "Yes, yes. This will be an interesting conquest. A city woman. I have had a few in my time, but the country ones are always far more willing. We just have to strike her at her most inner instincts." Grinning, Dionysus walked past the satyrs and nymphs as they stood up and started to follow him. "We will play a new tune tonight—a very alluring and strong one. She will not resist."

"That's the spirit of my lord," the satyr mused as they walked out to the fields to begin another session of lovemaking and wine debauchery.

That night, Aglaia was wide-awake, as the town slept peacefully. Her husband was sleeping soundly, snoring. She was a bit aggravated by his snoring; it was hours before she could get a decent sleep. It didn't help that she had to wake up in the morning and do all of that work. She wasn't used to having an entire day of gardening, making wine, and tending to farm animals.

Her husband wasn't a bad person. He had a good heart and actually treated her very well. She had been attracted to him when she met him. It was an arranged marriage. Her father married her to Agrios, thinking it would be a good match, that the country life was a more prosperous life. In many ways, it was and it was great to be out of the smelly and corrupt world she had known in Athens. Nature was kind and beautiful. Even so, a woman could get lonely out here. Everyone in the farming village was so helpful, supporting one another, but Aglaia still felt like an outsider.

She had thought over and over that day

about what her husband had told her about the secret world of Dionysus. It was just a walk away; it seemed right down that path. She wondered if he was teasing her. Did people really walk down there and never come back? No way, she thought with amusement. What a fairy tale. Did country folk really believe such superstitious stories so readily? She loved her husband, but couldn't help but think of what an ignorant fool he was. His thinking was so backward. Sure, she believed in the gods, but she couldn't believe in all of that.

Then, she heard the music.

It was different that the last few nights. The other few nights, it had been a little softer, calm, with the drifting sound of bagpipes and possibly some other instruments. This night, however, it was louder and sounded as if it could be a chorus. The tune was different too—as disorganized as the other sound was that she was used to hearing—this one seemed wilder. It was as if it were calling directly to her. She questioned her sanity. She doubted anyone else could hear this music that seemed to dance in her head with a taunting disjointed rhythm.

When she got out of the bed and walked up to the window, Aglaia could tell that the sound was coming from the path. There was no doubt. She started to crawl out of the window before even thinking or considering what she was doing. Before, she would just curiously listen. Now, she was stepping out and walking toward the field, toward the path, her thoughts suddenly set on a new world. She moved slowly, her rational mind popping up every now and then to question if this was really worth pursuing. Deep inside, she felt like she had already made her mind up. It was hard, tough to fight these feelings. Her heart ached. Her insides were shivering. Her pussy was hot and wet. She could even feel it dripping on her nightgown.

She couldn't fight it. The call was too strong.

At the mouth of the path, she felt her last moment to resist. Aglaia walked on, and unlike Lot's wife, she didn't look back. She couldn't look back. The divine had called her. Her insides were blossoming with the new needs of spring and soon, those desires would be fulfilled.

She had walked down that path for a mile; her senses bewildered. She often thought she was going to go insane—was this what it was like to see the gods, to experience their wonder? Her sexual energies going berserk, a strange inner goddess rising out of her, nature teasing her—sex—she could have had an orgasm right then and there. Every time she thought she was going to, however, she was back at square one, the root of her desire, as if on some continuous loop of rising and falling. Then, in the darkness, she saw him. She knew him at once as she bowed to the ground. It was a male, naked, with fiery eyes and an essence she had never encountered before. It was Dionysus.

"You have come." The lord smiled. "Finally, join us."

The woman rose to take the lord's hand as she looked about. She was surprised to see campfires formed all along a wide field covered with nymphs and satyrs. They were all intoxicated, some of them still drinking. Many were lying out in the grass, having sex with each other, satyrs riding nymphs and nymphs riding satyrs. Some of the satyrs chased teasing nymphs through the trees as they laughed and shouted. A number of the strange beings were near the fires, playing panpipes and beating on strange drums that the human woman had never seen before. Maybe these drums had travelled with the lord on his trips to Africa and other strange, remote parts of the world that she would never know.

After guiding Aglaia through the field, Dionysus took the woman to his throne. It was so simple and modest, but from the energy of the rocks and the grass, Aglaia knew that the spot was holy. The lord sat down on it and rested his hands on his knees, his legs spread out. Aglaia immediately got on her knees before the lord and prostrated. She had never thought that something like this would happen. All of her life, her people, her family, and everyone she had known worshiped this god with such vigor. They credited him with the prosperity of their businesses, the joy of life, and the basic needs of survival. She felt as if she had been guided by his force all this time.

The smell of sex filled the air. Aglaia felt

her body alive with desire, and at the same time, she was ashamed. How could she look at a deity in such a lustful way? It must have been sinful, wrong. Even a god that allowed the power of sex and energies beyond the rationality of the human soul to spring to life must have his limits. How could a woman like Aglaia appeal to his love without insulting him?

"Your lord," Aglaia began, "I'm honored to—"

Dionysus interrupted the woman with a deep and passionate kiss. He seemed to not be the one for conversation, or maybe he had finally gotten what he was looking for. The kiss made Aglaia nervous at first but then she felt at ease. She couldn't help but curse herself, feeling his tongue in her mouth, making her ooze deep down inside. That was when she felt like she could have melted. The heat inside of her body soon gave way as she was taken in by this strange god of a being. It wasn't long before her nightgown was ripped away that she was completely exposed to him. She felt her head being brought down to her cock.

The human moaned as the god's cock shoved itself into her mouth like a mere wine gourd needing a plug. It didn't stop with her lips or even the inside of her mouth, either. She could feel her throat getting penetrated, over and over again. Aglaia's hand reached down to her cunt. She knew that it was her time to serve the god and she felt a strong power requiring obligation and responsibility mixed with excitement and enjoyment.

The cock pulled out of her mouth, only teasingly, forcing Aglaia to say, "Allow me to service this cock, please." With that, the god shoved the cock back into the woman's mouth, going to work and plowing her. Dionysus smiled as the woman's tongue gripped him like a natural. He was pleased.

As the woman sucked his cock, Dionysus was granted a telepathic look into the woman's psyche. He could see her past, her present, and the future that awaited her—here with him. He saw her mere human past, worshipping him and always wanting to be with him. He saw her hard times before her marriage, her secret life as a prostitute in the streets of Athens, pleasuring men for sex. She would always pray to him before work, and by divine energy, he would answer without conscious focus, empowering her sexual sessions. Those sessions came from a need for money to support her family, a want to survive, and the wishes of a better life further down the path of life.

"I see you as you truly are, Aglaia," the god spoke as the woman sucked his cock submissively.

Aglaia started to cry in a mix of joy and shame as she sucked the holy cock, listening to his words as he pleased her mouth. She fingered herself more rapidly and intensely.

"Your husband would never know how to accept your strange and bewildered past," Dionysus said. "But I will. I will always accept you as you truly are—a product of nature. A living will of divine, continuous sex."

Aglaia gripped the god's knees as his cock handled her mouth. She could have sworn that he had grown so much inside of her.

"Allow me to offer this to you. I am a god of many pleasures. Your husband told you that no woman that has walked down that path has gone back. That is true. All of them chose to stay with me. But they did have a choice. No one is held back here beyond their own will."

Aglaia gagged many times but couldn't help not wanting to force the cock deeper down that neck of hers.

"So, Aglaia... Will you go back to your loving and humble husband? He loves you a great deal. I have taken many a woman from a man. Will you stay here with me? Will you know the eternal joys of sex and pleasure, here with me, my nymphs and my satyrs?"

"Mmmm. Mmmm." Aglaia responded so happily to the latter option.

Dionysus smiled. "I knew you would make the wise decision. Know that I love many and you are one of them now."

As Aglaia continued to suck the god's dick, she felt changes taking place within her. The sadness and mundane energies of the human life were leaving her—she felt more divine, more eternal. She had always been a beautiful woman, but now she felt perfect. Her skin was smoother, the eyes glowed, and even her lips felt more luscious and full. A strong sexual energy awakened inside of her. She felt the earth around her in a new way. She had an affinity with the grass, the rocks, and the far off streams and rivers in other parts of the mountains. In a matter of thirteen seconds, a more real self woke up inside of her. She had become a nymph.

She suckled that cock more and more as Dionysus face fucked her harder. Aglaia could feel the hands of other nymphs and satyrs on her. One of the satyrs started to ram her in the ass. Another nymph got under her and started to eat her out. A nymph and satyr started to suckle her nipples. This was a process of being made, her last identity destroyed, the human world a forgotten and unwanted mystery to her. The surrounding nymphs handling Aglaia felt their asses were being penetrated from behind, their crotches eaten by satyrs. This huge collection of beings was linked to each other like chains, providing sexual pleasure to each other. For a matter of hours, they stayed interlocked, fucking until they could get the approval of their lord.

They did. Dionysus shot a huge wad of silver elixir into the mouth of Aglaia. As he did, all of the beings, without fail, shifted to orgasm with him, pouring their juices in and on each other, on the ground, the rocks, the grass, and everything nearby. Light started to fill the field. It was morning.

All of the beings moved away from each other, taking places in the grass and trying to regain their strength and vitality. Some of them dozed off lazily to sleep. As everyone found their own place to settle, Aglaia sat at the knee of Dionysus, grasping his leg tightly. She looked up at him adoringly.

"My lord," Aglaia addressed politely. "What do we do now?"

Dionysus pressed a hand against his chin and sighed. "Find a satyr and have your fun if you wish."

Aglaia's eyes widened. "A satyr? But... but... my lord—I truly wish to stay here, by your side. I wish to pleasure you and make you happy."

Dionysus nodded. "That you did. You made me truly happy. But now, you are made. You wish to pleasure me and stay by my side like all the others. But now I have claimed you and I must find new things to focus my time upon." Patting the woman on her head, the god stood up and walked away from the stony throne, moving toward the path.

Aglaia almost followed the god but felt something leap up behind her and start to handle her asshole. She looked behind to see a horny satyr going to work. Sighing, Aglaia lay on the ground and took it willingly. Perhaps she could get used to this life.

"Aglaia?" Agrios kept calling out constantly that morning as he searched the hills. "Aglaia?"

"Poor guy," a man said to the wife as he

watched him move back and forth from a distance. "He lost his woman last night. I doubt he'll ever get her back. That happens often here you know."

"Yes," the wife said. "It's unfortunate. By the way, did you hear that weird music last night?"

5 DREAM STALKERS

Greg's insomnia had gotten the best of him for the past 3 days. He often wanted to retire early, away from the late night scenes of the city and into bed. But with this crippling sleep disorder, it was tough. The breeze of the night air could be a comfort in those early October nights so he left it open midway, feeling his bedroom cool down. With a simple blanket and a pillow, he laid down, trying to clear his thoughts and focus on sleeping.

As soon as he closed his eyes, Greg could feel his body becoming stiffer. He felt a bit lethargic for some reason as well, and all that manic energy he was used to feeling had dissipated. Relief flowed over him. In a moment's time, he was leaving behind all his thoughts and emotions that had been racing through him during the day. Some strange warmth came over him, making him feel pleasant and calm. It was as if he were being tranquilized by a sense of peace that had evaded him for years.

Suddenly, there was a knock at the door.

The sound startled Greg immediately, his back rising quickly and looking out towards the door. Surprisingly, instead of another knock coming from the door, Greg could see someone standing inside of his room right in front of the window. Although the figure was a little shadowy, he could make a female's curvaceous figure, long dark hair, and smooth skin. She had her hand on the windowsill, staring at Greg's direction.

"What do you want?" Greg said.

Instantly, Greg felt his body freezing again. He tried to scream but found his voice muffled completely. He looked towards the woman as she started to walk closer, her features more noticeable. There was nothing peculiar about her beautiful peach complexion, her long flowing hair and slender fingers as they reached out and touched his face. The only features that stood out as uncanny to Greg were the woman's eyes, orange orbs that seemed to pierce into his soul without hesitation. The woman's lips were soft with a texture of the sweetest fruit, enticing him.

Thoughts of protest did cross Greg's mind. Who was this woman to intrude into his apartment? How did she appear as mysteriously as he was entering sleep, possibly coming through a window that was so many stories up in the air? She couldn't have been human. Even as Greg tried to search for reason in this event, he gave up quickly. Those eyes were just way too compelling and strong. The woman leaned against his bed, her hands in his, looking deep into him.

"I," she said, "am a succubus."

Her plush lips kissed his; her eyes closed as she entered his mouth. Hands rubbed against the back of his head as she held him close, taking in his essence with soft breathes. Greg felt his eyes roll up in ecstasy. If he had time to think, he would have recognized the word succubus easily. He had read of these things before, the female demons that traveled when man slept, having sex with them. In that strong sense of desire exploding through his body and the sensual feeling of the woman's hand against his cock, however, Greg had nothing to think about. He could only feel and find himself wanting more.

"People say that we are bad," the succubus said with a pout. "My sisters have been persecuted and hated. We are not demons." She leaned in and kissed again. "We are goddesses. We are queens of the night. We are immortal. Let me please you." With that, the woman climbed up on the bed and over Greg, holding him down as her hands massaged his shoulders.

Greg gritted his teeth. This felt so good. He could feel her pulling the blankets away from him, pulling down his pants and pulling out his cock. It was then that he realized that she had been naked the whole time. He had seen her when she came up and saw her hard nipples in the night air, but it just hadn't registered. The strange shock of a stranger invading his home was now replaced with the overwhelming sense of a beautiful maiden bearing gifts. Her breasts were so naturally big. They didn't look like inflated balloons, not like his ex-wife who had left him behind for a Hollywood career. No, these were the real deal. They were nice and plump. It surprised him when, even though he was frozen, the succubus grabbed his hands and helped him grab them. It was as if she was telepathic and could hear everything on his mind.

"You've never felt anything quite like that, have you human?" the succubus said with a teasing grin.

She had already mounted him. His hardened cock was already implanted into her gushing wet cunt. He could tell that she liked to run the show. With her hands on his shoulders and his hands on her breasts, she was getting to work. The rocking motions of her hips were pushing against his cock with all of the strength that she could muster. She was such a strong woman. Greg didn't even feel insecure as his more frail body supported her, her legs brushing up against his skin. Damn! She was such a powerhouse. He noticed that the more she rocked against his cock, the faster she was getting in her motions. She didn't even wasted a breath.

Greg moaned. "Damn!" He thought. She was really working hard for this. It was as if she was trying to break him in the fastest way that she could. He really liked it. He couldn't even think of giving her pleasure. It was as if she was doing this all for him, giving him the pleasure that he needed, just so she could make him cum. Part of his mind wanted to resist so he could make this last longer and get as much out of having a lovely night visitor to the best of his ability. With all of the time that he did have, however, he had to make this last.

Breaking out in sweat, Greg felt his hand slipping a bit on the succubus' breast. Still, she never left him. Her breasts stayed in his sweaty, needing hands. He really wanted to get into her as deep as he could, and he could already feel his entire dick swallowed into her cunt. His balls swung helplessly below as she seemed to fuck him in a hyper-speed motion. He was surprised she had been moving fast at first, but it seemed she had reached this superhuman speed in a quick moment of time. The feeling got him really hot.

"Please," Greg said, surprising himself that he could speak again. She must have been giving him permission to. She controlled everything. "Don't stop!"

"It won't stop until you stop, my love," the succubus said with a smile. She continued to ride him with harsh and rapid motions. "You just must meet my sisters. Here are some more succubae."

The sisters appeared instantly in the room, their bodies just as natural and lush as the first one. They had brought in a sweet smell of vanilla and honey. Maybe they bathed in it. When they approached, their hair seemed to hold an aroma of rosemary incense. For possibly demonic beings, they sure were pretty and possessed a beautiful smell. God! Greg wanted to fuck them. How could he even concentrate on just one?

Greg was surprised he hadn't cum yet. He felt like he was completely in the first succubus' orders. Perhaps he couldn't cum until she gave him the red light magically. The sisters leaned down on the bed with the pair. As the first succubus fucked Greg's dick without mercy, the other succubae kissed him up and down his chest. They played with his hair, kissed him, and giggled as if they were going gaga over him. It made Greg feel really good. It had been a while since he had gotten this much attention from women.

His cock throbbed in the succubus's clit. The clit's muscles squeezed against his cock as if it wanted to milk him for all the sperm he had. What would happen to him when this was done? He had seen the stories of succubus draining their male partners, taking their life force. Was he going to die this way? He honestly didn't care at this point. He just wanted to cum in this woman really badly. If he could do that, it would be all he needed to fulfill his life.

"That's all you want, isn't it?" Greg asked, struggling to speak. "My seed..."

The succubae giggled.

Greg groaned as he felt his cock throbbing faster. He was getting closer. The head of his cock was gapping pretty wide as he felt cum rising to the top. It wasn't long before it was shooting like a whale's blowhole and sending wet chrome drops into the woman's open cunt. Her juices were flooding his lap as she moaned, feeling the cum enter her as she slowed down her motions. Semen was filling her up. Greg could feel a strong suction from her pussy, too. It was as if her cunt was drinking up all that she could from Greg's nocturnal emission.

Greg was sweating and panting as the succubus got up. She walked to the center of the room, taking a finger and licking up the cum that was left on the outside of the cunt. Greg looked at her as she turned towards him and smiled.

"My turn," the second succubus said. She was a long legged woman with curly blonde hair. Her eyes were the same as her sister's though her skin was a little fairer. She had a flower resting in her ear.

"W...wait," Greg said as he looked at the woman with shock. "So... so soon?"

The woman said nothing as she pulled up and mounted herself onto Greg's cock. He was surprised as he felt aroused again. Though he would never admit it in a million years, his past experiences with sex had always been short. It didn't take him long to cum and he was usually knocked out after one nut. He couldn't imagine having this other succubus fuck him right after he had fucked another one. Even so, he could feel it about to happen again, his cock just as erect and excited as it was with the first sister. The woman mounted as the sisters watched, their arms folded with intense pupils watching the scene calmly.

"Wait, please... give me time. Give me..." Greg gritted his teeth as the succubus rode him. His cock was kind of hurting. This second time was not starting out as pleasurable as the first time. He was still feeling the effects of that super brisk ride the first succubus had given him. Never had his cock hurt so much. Still, it was a bit pleasurable, the excitement still there. The woman's cunt was a little tighter but still as slippery and wet. He could tell she was experienced in riding too. Almost effortlessly, she held him down under her, having his cock slide inside of her cunt, licking her lips deviously as she worked to get her fill.

"Damn! Please stop. Please." Greg couldn't resist though he wanted to. He knew that he could only talk again for the succubae's amusement. They were going to fuck and destroy him, he thought to himself. He couldn't help but think it now. All those memories of stories he read. These things may have felt good, but they never ended well. The woman's cunt smelled so good, filling the cool air. The attention got him going, her eyes staring into his, seeming to burn right through his skull. He couldn't resist this. There was no way. Her hands were rubbing against his side. Her motions were so fast and harsh against him. He could even feel as her nails dug a bit into his side.

"Ohhh god..." Greg said as he came again.

It happened so quickly. The woman got off of him and then the third one slipped on again. They didn't let him protest or speak this time. He could only move his mouth slowly, attempting to voice words. He felt like a puppet, held at the whim of these sisters as they rode him, controlled his orgasms and his pleasures. His hard-on wasn't even allowed to go down for this sister. Her pussy was the tightest, the most slick; gripping onto his cock was an enclosed pressure. It wasn't long before he could hear her moan. It was the first convincing moan of pleasure he had heard that night.

She was taking her time with him. Maybe she knew how her sisters could be. Maybe she was having pity for him. Although it wasn't a tortoise's speed, it wasn't too fast for a human. She moved her hands through her long brown hair, moaning as she bobbed up and down on Greg, her tits bouncing in the air as her shiny nipples danced in the moonlight. Greg felt a tear roll down on his cheek. This was so pleasurable, so beautiful, and he was so happy.

Her pussy was dripping everywhere. He could feel her liquids mixing with the other sister's wet fluids stained on his cock and pubic hairs. Greg hoped this would last for a while. His cock was already throbbing something heavy. He felt like he could explode any minute.

"God," one of the sisters said. "Would you hurry it up already?"

"Yeah," the other one said, "we got a long night ahead of us. Can't spend it all night here."

"You guys get all the fun," the succubus said as she continued to fuck the helpless human. "I just get sloppy thirds." Ramming harder on Greg, her pussy muscles squeezed against him violently.

Greg was surprised by the increase of motion. It was fierce but satisfactory. It felt so good. He didn't even notice the blood trickling under him. The woman was moving faster and faster. Greg felt like he could explode any moment. He had never been so happy in his life.

It was then that he really did feel himself explode in the most intense orgasm he ever experienced. Greg didn't even notice the injury caused to his cock as he spit his last squirts of semen he would ever be able to produce. His balls hung limp as the woman was filled with the last precious drops. She slowly lifted off of Greg, allowing him to drift off to sleep.

The women stood over the man, musing over him like a painting.

"He was fun," the first one said.

"A bit of a bore," said the second.

"I don't know," the third one said. "He was kind of cute."

The three started to walk to the window. The second sister came to a stop, making the other sisters hesitate as well.

"Tell me," the second one started, "what's so special about this one? Why don't we just drain the living life out of him? Sure, we got enough sperm to lay demon eggs for weeks, but I don't ever feel right leaving a job without getting it done completely."

The first one shrugged. "I don't know. There's something heavily pathetic about this human's life. I like draining some wealthy old fuck or some smug superstar bastard. These regular guys can't really hold a torch to that kind of excitement."

"You're the boss," the second one replied.

"Hey," the third one said calmly, her eyes flashing. "I just thought of the perfect person to drain. My cunt's still throbbing. Let's go."

"Let's," the other two confirmed.

As the three left quietly, Greg slept soundly in his bed. It was the best sleep he had ever had in years, and it would make a very painful morning worth it.

6 LILITH

Harold held onto his last cigarette with a lingering pinch, watching it slowly burn. He needed to savor this last cigarette as he drank his beer, drowning his sorrows before he would have to go home.

Living in the uptown was hard. There were many responsibilities for one in Harold's position. Under the dim lights of the lonely bar he had wandered into for the evening, he could escape a little bit. This was the place that he had heard, all of his life, not to go. Maybe a sense of life could reenergize him for his painful life that would resume in the morning.

The place was a little hole in the wall on the outskirts of downtown. It was so late that even the jukebox had been shut down. There were two really intimidating guys playing pool. There was another other weird-looking patron on the other side of the bar.

He was drinking out of a bottle all by himself. There must have been five empty bottles near his new one.

"Get me another one, please," Harold said to the bartender. The burly bartender nodded calmly before going for another beer nozzle, refilling Harold's mug. As he looked over the bartender's face, Harold could only think of how rough and dismal the man's features were. Maybe he was just another lost soul, working his life away like Harold. Was there really a difference between the upper and lower parts of the city?

"We don't get your types often," the bartender said as he looked at Harold's suit, tie, and trench coat. His eyes had a bit of disgust. "You from uptown?"

Harold nodded. "Yes. Yes, I am." Harold reached for the mug and downed another drink. "I came down here for business."

The bartender chuckled, his chin like a sanded down rock. "What kind of business? Drugs? Women? You must have a lot of balls coming down here."

"I doubt it." Harold was already slamming an empty mug on the counter. "Now can I have another, please?"

The bartender laughed a little as he reached for the mug and filled it up again. "I thought your types weren't supposed to drink."

Harold didn't want to talk to the bartender anymore. He had seen him sizing him up since he came in the door. Maybe this was a seedier part of the city, nearly like a ghost town with the exception of all the possible rift raft of the night stalking the alleyways and broken down tenements. There wasn't any sense of fear or dread facing such a reality for Harold. He had come from modest beginnings; he knew these areas were rough. His family worked their way to where they were now. His father was sitting on his own fortune. Harold had a sister living clearly halfway across the world, travelling and doing whatever she wanted.

His brother Mikey was the reason he had come down here. Mikey used to live uptown years ago. At one time, his life was filled with corporate employee of the month awards and company picnics. Those days were over. He was a fallen angel now, a drug dealer, living amongst the barbaric and devilish underworld of the downtown area. This was an area that Mikey had plenty of business, traffic moving in and out, day and night. For a moment, when the bartender was harassing him, he nearly asked him if he knew who Mikey was. Maybe then, he would know that Harold wasn't a safe man to play games with. That might have squashed any trouble that could come his way.

Just then, as if there was a magnet with an attractive pull at the door, Harold stared towards the front of the bar. That was when he saw one of the most pleasing items to ever grace his eye. There was a woman. Her legs were long and bear under a tight red short skirt, her high heels a matching scarlet. What a beauty. The woman was tall, inches above Harold's height, though shorter than the bartender. She had a peach complexion, a tan that looked far too natural and clean for a city girl. Still, the attitude in her movie vixen face, her confident strut, and shiny brown eyes seemed to wear the influence of the streets. Her bust was stuck out round and shapely. Her breasts stood out heavy in her top as long reddish hair dropped down her slender cheekbones and past her shoulder blades.

As the woman approached the bar, Harold couldn't help but to get a good look at the woman's backside. It stuck out smoothly, and yet it was so firm and well-proportioned with her fit body. She looked to the bartender with mascara-lined eyes. "You know my usual, Sam."

"No one would forget your usual, doll," the bartender said before reaching for a glass.

The woman laughed with a hand over her breasts. "Oh, you would be surprised how often many do. Let alone a girl's name."

The bartender mixed the woman's drink. It was quite a loaded concoction.

Harold stared at the woman with some low and shy glances. She was reaching into her purse and pulling out a pack of cigarettes. Thank goodness, he thought in relief, at least she's a smoker. Harold didn't want to feel like too much of a loser nearby this bombshell. His heart melted a bit as the woman stuffed her cigarette in her mouth and started to puff away. Drinking and smoking. These were things an uptown girl would never do.

Before long, Harold had adjusted his chair a bit closer to the woman. There was a bit of shame as he saw the woman give a muted giggle in response to his movement.

"I could try to remember your name," Harold said nervously, "if you allowed me to."

The woman looked toward Harold, staring into his eyes with an amused smile. "Oh?"

Harold stared back sheepishly.

Placing her glass down, the woman held out a hand. "I'm Lilith."

Harold stared at the hand a bit before chuckling awkwardly, reaching out and sharing it. "Name's Harold. Harold."

"Just Harold?"

Harold's eyes seemed to shake a bit as he pulled back a tad bit. "Yeah. And you. Just Lilith?"

"We don't have to know each other's last names," the woman said as she turned toward the bar with a smirk, puffing a cigarette.

"I know where this is going," the bartender mused as he walked to another side of the bar.

"You know," Harold began with a slight stutter, "I've seen a lot of beautiful women before, but you have to be the most beautiful I've ever seen. It's not easy for me to compliment someone, I must admit. It's just that—"

"It's just that you didn't expect to see a woman as beautiful as me in a place like this."

Harold blinked, frozen. "Well, that's not

exactly what I was going to say, honestly, but, yes—it's true."

"Of course it's true. Look. Uh, what's your name again, Bob?"

"It's Harold."

"Okay. Look, Harold. What do you think about my ass?"

Harold looked at the woman's backside quickly before looking back up at her. "Well, it's very lovely—a beautiful ass."

The woman rolled her eyes. "Oh, come on. Tell me how you really feel."

Harold fell silent.

"Don't you want to just... slap it?"

The bartender walked by with some bottles for the trash, grinning.

"No, I wouldn't want to—"

"Slap it." The woman grabbed Harold's hand and made him slap it. Hard. Harold found his hand wasn't leaving after the slap. As if mindlessly, he was grabbing her ass cheek, holding onto it and admiring its feel, its firmness.

A tear peaked at the corner of Harold's eye.

"You work too hard, Harold. I can tell. You need more fun in your life." The woman bent down and leaned over Harold, whispering into his ear. "So... tell me, Harold. Got a woman?"

Harold looked down at the ground. "Well, yes, I do. I'm married."

"Oh, that's a shame." The woman looked at Harold's hands. "But I don't see any rings."

"I like to take it off from time to time. She

does, too."

"Oh. Things going sour?"

Harold looked up at the woman. Why did he feel so compelled to be honest with her? "Yes."

"Yes. Of course." Lilith stood closer to Harold, her hands on her hips in a stance that was quite heroic. "Well, let me explain myself to you, Harold. You have problems. I solve them. That's why I'm here. That's why you came here."

Harold's eyes squinted a little. He was confused. "Wait—I came here looking for someone. Someone else, and... not in the way you think I would meet you. I came to meet a family member, and—"

"You're rambling, Harold. Rambling. Just relax."

Harold sighed, his shoulders hanging. "I'm sorry, it's just that... well, anyway... why are you here?"

"For exactly the thing that you are going through. I'm here for you. Here to release you from your shackles, your bonds, your worthless existence that you call life—if only for a night."

Harold froze again. "You're a prostitute?"

The woman laughed. It wasn't a little, pitying laugh. It was a boisterous laugh. Her hands were still on her hips, making her once heroic stance now seem a bit domineering, even degrading. She looked back to Harold as she licked her lips. "No, Harold. I don't sell myself. I would never sell myself. I believe in free love, baby."

"Free... love?"

"Yes. Free love. That's why I come here, to this bar. Without fail, I find something good. Every night, dear. It just happens that tonight, I found you.

Harold trembled as the woman's hand brushed his face.

Lilith pressed against Harold, her breathe so minty and pleasing but hot. "I confess— I'm used to more... rough men." Moving behind the businessman, Lilith started to massage his shoulders. "Guys like you, they usually don't come down here. They're scared shitless, trying to walk the straight and narrow, all that corporation bullshit. Still, I must admit that it turns me on to look at you. I always like something a little different. You look smart, sophisticated—I bet you have all sorts of secret desires you've wanted to explore but just couldn't."

Harold found himself breathing more heavily. "Why do you figure that?"

"Harold baby... please. Wife at home? Out all by yourself in this big, bad side of town? You're looking for a way out. You're looking for the ultimate in release. I can give that to you."

Harold was starting to give in more. He already allowed his head to drop against the woman's breast as she moved a hand through his hair. He couldn't help but hide his blushing face, though he was glad the dimming of the lights didn't allow his full pathetic state to be seen. The bulge in his tight pants was already becoming a burden.

The bartender was back near the lovebirds. He leaned towards Harold with a smile. "I see you like my girlfriend, stranger."

Harold's eyes got big as he eased up from Lilith. "Really? She's yours? Oh, I'm sorry, I didn't know. Please, I—"

The bartender laughed. "Ha ha. Calm down. She told you she likes free love, didn't she? Who am I to hold her on a leash?" The bartender slapped the man on his back. "If anything, she holds me on a leash!"

The woman raised a finger towards the bartender. "Watch it."

Continuing to smile, the bartender looked benevolently at the shaking businessman. "You want to have your little fun, right? Well, by all means. Have your fun." The bartender lifted his hand up and jingled some keys. "Take her to the back room. Get a little comfortable."

Harold stared at the keys. "This doesn't cost anything?" The man was nervous. This had to be a setup. Was he going to get robbed?

"Come on, man." The bartender laughed. "Anyone that looked in your eyes could tell you don't have anything coming your way like this in a while. Fuck your eyes. Anyone can look at you period and tell you couldn't get an opportunity like this."

Harold sighed. He looked back at Lilith. Wow, she really was pretty. She was teasing him too, looking in his direction with sad, puppy dog eyes.

"Look," Harold said, "I really got to go. I got my wife at home. She knows I stay out sometimes on business but... I'm not really the bar type. I just got kind of stressed out and stayed too long. I used to be an alcoholic and kept it secret. I quit for a good while but maybe—"

"Hush!" Lilith shouted. "Always with the talking!" Wrapping her arms around him, Lilith slipped her tongue into Harold's mouth. She held him so close and tight before his timid hands held her too, pressing his own tongue into her. He rubbed her down, bringing her closer as he inhaled deeply. Her scent was so sweet to him, her red hair brushing into his face as he suddenly felt her hand reach and slip into his pants. Was this even allowed here? He started to move a hand towards to try to fight it all, to protest, but it was hard to. It felt so good. He couldn't remember the last time that he had ever gotten such sexual attention, and then the memory hit him. Oh yeah. He never had such attention before, not even once in his life.

"That's enough," the bartender said. He jiggled the key's again as his head motioned towards the backdoor of the bar.

Harold grabbed the keys. He looked back at the bartender's strange stare, both cold and reinforcing, before feeling Lilith's hand grab his. She led the way, though it was not very far. Harold undid the doorknob keyhole and they were in.

There were no comfortable beds. No foldout cushions or mushy beanbags. The room was filled with a few pool tables and some supplies. The air seemed stuffy.

The door closed and shut.

"Now Harold," Lilith said as she undid her top and revealed her juicy boobs. "You're going to have to satisfy me." She leaned against him with a finger on his chest. "And when I say satisfy me, I mean fuck me. Fuck me hard, strong, and without remorse."

Harold bit his lip. "I'll... I'll try.

Harold's pants dropped to the ground without warning when Lilith undid his belt. She threw the belt to the ground, pulling the underwear to Harold's knees. Harold, wanting to impress, reached around Lilith's waist and pulled down her skirt. Before long, they were both removing the rest of each other's articles of clothing, one by one.

A naked Lilith pushed Harold's nude body against the edge of one of the pool tables. She didn't laugh at the relatively less than normal size of Harold's throbbing erection. "We're going to do this standing up a bit. Now, rule number one—I always ride on top." Lilith pulled up over Harold, bending her knees a little and stuffing what she could of Harold's cock inside of her.

Wow, Harold thought, this was so awkward. As strange as it all was, however, Harold would not give up this opportunity. He gave himself like a willing slave to the woman. He felt her cunt wrap around his cock. She was moving herself up and down the best way she could on him. She was holding him, forcing him to help with the motions too.

Harold didn't want to be insecure anymore. His insecurities got him a lousy marriage, a stressful job, and all sorts of trouble. No—tonight, he wanted to be sexy. He wanted to be desirable. He wanted to be wanted. There was nothing in the world he had ever wanted more, and tonight, he would go for his private dream.

He groaned a bit as he realized the cunt was starting to fit better. Had he grown inside of her? His cock was beginning to stretch her walls. She was even moaning! He never heard his wife moan—just sigh. Lilith was no fish like his wife—she was moving, vibrant and lively. Harold could also swear that he was growing in height. Once, where he felt like an amazon was trying to do the impossible by mounting his cock, Harold's feet were more supported on the ground. He was holding Lilith with more ease. Eye to eye, face to face, he was standing opposite from her.

My, how he had grown.

His body was stronger. He could support the woman better. She was moaning, crying, and they weren't even lying down. He picked her up and pinned her to the nearby wall. Ramming into her, he grunted. Her sweat was starting to fall into his face. So strange. He felt like he was on top of the world. What a weird, weird woman. What was she doing to him?

"That's it... big boy!" Lilith gritted her teeth and sucked in air fiercely, riding over the man's cock. He wasn't the same nerd that had wandered into the bar that evening. No. He was reborn, anew, and fresh.

"I'm going to need you, baby," Lilith said breathily, "to get me off."

The movements were becoming swifter. Harold's cock was being squeezed by the woman's cunt with force. She was panting, begging for more. Harold wondered how much more he could give her. Could he satisfy her right? Would he make her cum?

He had never made a woman orgasm before. The thought really excited him.

"Oh yes! Keep going, keep going." Lilith's red hair whipped her partner in the face. Her hands were gripping his back hard. It was then that Harold realized how long Lilith's fingernails were. They were scratching against his back, soft at first, nearly rubbing. As she continued to rock up and down over his cock, however, her nails started to dig deeper into the flesh of his back. It was noticeable and there was a sting, but at the same time, Harold didn't mind. He had become some sort of super-human, able to take more pain than he had ever taken before. As she scratched at him, he could feel some blood oozing down his back. His newly found leg muscles stretched as he supported the woman. His hands supported her legs as his arms strained. Lilith's head moved back as her hair continued to whip, her mouth letting out ungodly sounds.

"What have you done to me," Harold said with a gritty voice. "Whatever you've made me... this isn't normal."

As Harold forked his cock into Lilith, he could feel, even hear, her wet liquids pouring onto the floor in splatter. Her sex was filling the room with a pungent odor. Harold was surprised that he wasn't disgusted.

"Oh Harold," Lilith said breathily as she held his back with nails more reminiscent of talons. "You shall dearly love your service in hell."

Harold's mind didn't even race. The word hell just sat in his mind for a moment, meaningless at first, and soon become clearer. Hell. Somehow, he had come to hell. This wasn't a glorious act at all. This sex was actually enjoyable. The woman actually liked them. No, this was nothing like the paradise Harold's corporation preached about. Had he been deceived? He didn't feel like he had been trapped, or even misled. Somehow, he chose this. Somehow, he felt this was right.

The woman started to slam herself harder and harder against Harold's upright penis. He was surprised. For a woman that was being supported in his arms and against the wall, she really did seem to take control of the situation. The whole time he thought that she had granted him some insane transference of energy so that he could be in control, but no, she was in control. She had been in control all this time. Harold had become strong but Lilith was stronger. Her leg muscles were so pronounced as she squeezed against Harold's skin, riding him, taking his throbbing and thick cock that had grown so long and heavy. She was controlling it, making it take the abuse her cunt was dishing out on it with each falling action. The cunt was bleeding from the friction.

"As soon as you came downtown," Lilith moaned, "you entered Hell."

Harold gritted his teeth as, suddenly, without warning, he climaxed inside Lilith. It was as if she made him do it.

"You left the upper world to come to the lower world." Lilith said, no longer panting or moaning, even as she continued to ride the ejaculating dick. "It is better for a man to rule in Hell than to serve in Heaven, some say."

Harold spit the last of his cum into Lilith's vagina. He buried his face in her boobs as he still pinned her to the wall. "I've... I've heard that before."

"Yes. Unfortunately for you, or possibly fortunate, Harold dear, you rule nothing here."

Harold backed away from Lilith, pulling his cock out of her. She seemed to slowly float towards the ground calmly. Harold felt disoriented as he backed up a little.

"I now own you, Harold. Just like every last man in this bar. Just like anyone who comes into the downtown. This is my territory."

Harold laughed. If he hadn't had such a bizarre sex section, he wouldn't have believed anything this crazy chick was telling him. "Oh. And the bartender. Next thing you're going to tell me is that he's Satan and you're his bride, huh?"

Lilith laughed. "Oh, you are so smart, aren't you? Don't you know Satan is just a word meaning enemy... adversary?"

Suddenly, Harold felt the pain shoot through his back. His eyes squinted, his teeth clenched as he tried to bar it. It was horrible.

"Well, consider me your adversary. Consider me your Satan."

Harold felt the strength within his body giving out. He noticed that he was shrinking. Blood was shooting from his back.

"Wait. My wife. She's waiting for me."

"You don't deserve the life you had in Heaven, Harold. You strayed from your vows. You strayed from your pact."

Harold was crying now. The pain was shooting through him. His body felt little tremors rising and falling beneath his flesh. A horrid jagged feeling shot through his cock as it shrunk along with him back to his normal size.

The cock exploded, sending Harold to scream. Lilith liked this very much. Her horrid laughter filled the room.

Harold could hear screams and yelps all around the room. His eyes glanced about to see faces and hands shooting from the walls and ceilings, the floors, the pool tables. No. She didn't lie. This was hell. This was really hell.

He looked to his left. In the wall, tortured among other bodies, was a familiar face. It was almost identical to Harold. It was screaming and writhing in agony. Harold had no doubt it was his brother.

"Mikey? Mikey!"

"Oh yes." Lilith grinned wide as her eyes glowed. Huge black wings formed on her back. "He was delicious."

Harold started pleading, falling on his knees as he looked at the strange being with immense fear. "Please. Let me go. I'll pay you. I'll—"

"You've paid me enough with your unadulterated loyalty! With that, I am thankful." Lilith gave a teasing smile as her wings flapped. She hovered towards Harold and started biting into him.

Harold's screams carried on for a few hours.

After her meal, Lilith stepped back into the main bar room. The bartender was standing behind the bar, his horns prominent, as the other three patrons had revealed their demonic personas as well.

"Was he delicious, mistress?" the bartender asked in some weird, ethereal voice as his eyes were now spinning black holes.

"Oh, Samuel" Lilith said with an elated expression, "he was divine."

The morning brought a brand new sunny day. A modest office in the tallest high-rise greeted the sun from the windows. It was the office for the president of a very important incorporation. An old man in a suit played putt golf with a little display he set up in the center of the room.

A knock sounded at his door.

"Come in," the old man said as he glanced up.

The door opened. It was a beautiful woman in a business suit, her hair neatly combed, not too long or short. In her hands was a newspaper. "Daily paper, Lord."

The old man nodded as he walked forward. "Oh. Oh, yes. Thank you."

As he took the paper, the woman walked out, closing the door respectfully. The old man thumbed through the paper—there were so many good things happening in the uptown. His employees did such good work.

Suddenly, the old man had an idea. Walking to his teleprompter, he pressed a button down. "Sarah, please send Harold in here."

Sarah answered back, "I'm sorry, sir, but Harold hasn't come in for the day yet."

The old man's brow rose up as he pressed the button again. "That's strange. Harold is never late. He's one of my best angels, you know."

"I know, Lord," the woman responded. "Maybe he got caught up in traffic or something."

"Hmmm. Who's to really know, these days, with these young people?"

With that, the Lord continued his game of putt putt. He had to admit, he was a little worried. If anything went wrong, it would be bad for business. People didn't like corporate or political corruption, at least that's what the documentaries seemed to suggest. After reasoning that it really wasn't worth it to think about such things, he grabbed a cigar out of his coat and puffed it lightly. Hopefully, Harold would be back with the drugs he promised that afternoon.

The newspaper fell to the floor. The Lord picked it up. It had landed on an interesting page. There was a woman with long red hair, long legs, and very lovable tits. Nearby her face was an advertisement for a bar downtown.

"Hello beautiful," the Lord said. "Guess I know where I'm going tonight."

—END—

7 TOY

The night had come quickly and it seemed unreasonably dark for such an early hour. Jason stood on the side of the road smoking a cigarette and reminiscing about the past. His mind raced through a catalogue of old lovers he had met right here, in the downtown area, while going out for a coffee or a simple walk. There was Cynthia the hairstylist, Mary the dancer, Stephanie, Heather, Alicia... after a while he lost count and forgot names. So many women had made their way into his life in the busy and dirty streets of the Big City. Even with his luck and the styles of a natural Casanova, he couldn't shake the fact that the older he was getting, the lonelier he felt.

"Those were some good times," Jason reassured his own ears as he took another drag of his cigarette, watching the cars go by.

The words of his friends flooded his mind. Advice from old romancers that never wanted to get locked down with a family or responsibilities always gave him the edge on picking up dates. He didn't really care for the domestic types. He liked the wild ones, the streetwalkers that offered pussy for free and mean walkers with nice, long legs that could be idolized in museums through photographs and painted pictures. Maybe that was why he was also such a great artist or at least why many people had told him that he was. If anyone that attended his shows knew that he came down here, on the seedy side of town, with hawk eyes nailed to the streets in silent vigil, they probably wouldn't be surprised. With the dark and urban sex scenes he incorporated into his work, everything would click to an observer like clockwork.

Even so, the painter still kept his travels to the ghetto and his many rendezvous there a deeply buried secret, except with those that were close to him. Other conquistadors and hungry thrill seekers that could share stories would give him some inspiration from their own trips down the dirty neighborhoods harboring porn stores, stripper huts, and X-rated movie theaters. Some of the hunters were artists just like Jason, and others were bankers, accountants, and heavy rollers with suspicious occupations that they would never really reveal. It didn't matter to Jason as long as they brought good stories from experiences and ideas of what he could try, if he hadn't thought of it yet.

The streets were particularly cold that night. Jason didn't mind that much. Honestly, he liked the cold better than the hot. The summer had been unpredictably kind for the citizens of Big City, who were used to the wind, so he was thankful that the autumn time had brought things back to normal. Now he could do his regular stalking of the streets comfortably with a snug jacket over his torso and a well-fitted cap on his shaved head. He rubbed his hands back and forth as he walked the blocks, seeing some women that looked fuck worthy. Still, he had high expectations and didn't want to end up with a crack whore or an unrespectable bitch. At times, he reasoned himself to be a connoisseur that could tell, just by looking, who was a gold digger, who had class, who didn't, and who would be a whiner, a bitch, a slut, or a queen that would dwarf him in superiority. At times, Jason's female friends would jokingly tell him how misogynistic he was, or disrespectful as a human being, but he couldn't help it. Maybe he got it from his father, the man he had gotten his romancing skills from, or maybe it was just the way his repressive anger came out as an artist and searcher for pussy.

Whatever, he said, leaving everything up for life to decide.

"You there!" a voice said behind him. It was quite a demanding male voice. "Hey man, turn around!"

Jason turned around to see a very dapper yet colorfully dressed male wearing purple pants with a matching jacket and hat. A golden cane was in his hand. Jason quickly recognized the man as a pimp.

Immediately rolling his eyes as he turned back around, Jason said, "Not interested."

"Hey, wait a second man!" The pimp walked up to Jason and pressed a hand on his back. "You haven't even heard what I've said yet, and you're dismissing me like I'm some random jerkoff?"

Jason gave a scoffing laugh. "You are some random jerkoff. I would be thankful if you didn't touch me, please."

The pimp pulled his hand back. "What? You got issues with space or something?"

"I just don't know where your hands have been is all."

The pimp chuckled, his smile wide as he pressed both of his hands against the handle of his cane and knocked. "Hey, okay man. Say, you're alright. You're quite alright. You know what? Fuck it. I understand. I respect you as a man." The pimp walked in front of Jason as he noticed him started to walk away. "But listen to my proposition before you go off like that."

Jason breathed a heavy sigh before looking the pimp into the face. "Look, man. I'm going to give it to you straight because I don't like bullshit. First of all, I don't need to pay for pussy—"

"Wait, wait, wait! Who said anything about having to pay for pussy, man? I didn't say that. Did I say that once at all? Hell! No, man, I'm not trying to sell you pussy. I got some good pussy for you for free!"

Jason looked the man in his face. "Good pussy for free?"

The man nodded his head.

Jason shook his head. "You're not making any sense, man. Now I think you're either trying to scam me or you're fucking crazy and wasting my time."

The pimp pressed his hand against Jason's chest again, trying to hold him in place before he walked off. The constant touching was irritating Jason, but he stopped anyway. He didn't like drama and although he wanted to keep looking for some women, he didn't feel too above hearing what the pimp had to say.

"Look, man—what I've got pays itself. I tried her once and ever since, it's been all I need. Everyone that I refer to her ends up feeling the same way, too. Look." The pimp reached into his pocket and pulled out a photograph. He handed it to Jason.

Jason grabbed the photo and inspected it carefully. The woman in the photograph was kind of strange and freaked him out a bit. She wore a weird blank mask and was sitting in a dark room filled with frilling curtains and a bed that looked like it could have come from Victorian England. At the same time, she had a body that Jason had never seen before and it enticed him immediately. He saw her soft and full bosoms as her nipples were noticeably perk and quite delectable. Her legs were crossed all ladylike, as if guarding a really sweet pleasure. She was slender yet juicy, her thighs and calves quite strong. Even her long hair flowed over the shoulders in a seductive way. With her hands rested on the bed, it seemed as if she was calling Jason, wanting him all to herself before even meeting him.

Jason had to look up from the photo and back to the pimp. "Wow, man... this is intense!"

The pimp just smiled and nodded. Jason couldn't tell if the smile was a shared sexual giddiness or some dark evil reaction to Jason being hit hook, line, and sinker. Either way, Jason was definitely hooked.

Shaking his head, Jason gave a strong look to the pimp's eye, not wanting to look like a chump. "Either way, man—how much are you selling this whore for?"

The pimp shook his head. "As I said, the girl is not for sale. She's free. And it's not me who chooses who she has her fun with. She chooses. And as soon as I saw you, she said that she wanted you."

Jason was about to protest, his finger rose in the air, when suddenly he felt a strange sensation in his head. He rubbed the back of his head, feeling a sudden chase of vertigo. It hit quickly, leaving him confused as the world around him seemed to swirl and disappear in a maze. What was going on? He didn't know. If anything, he wanted to get out and back on the streets, but the surrounding neighborhoods with its cars and sex stores had dissolved and transformed into something else. Everything had become more closed in, less spacious, though still a bit comfortable. It was still dark however, but what was no longer the city was a strange, Victorian-styled room. The room was the room of the photograph, and on the bed before Jason was the woman that he saw in the photograph, mask and all.

Shaking his head in disbelief, Jason held back a little, staring the woman up and down. "Who the hell are you?"

The woman stretched out on the bed, her legs folded just like the photograph as she tossed some hair from her shoulders. "A toy."

"Toy?"

"I'm just a toy. Not Toy. A toy. The toy you will be playing with this evening. Pleased to meet you."

Jason felt some fear take over him but he kept his cool. He didn't want to jump to conclusions, and he doubted that he could get out of this situation so quickly. "So tell me, lady—you must not be the one that's quick to give out names, I guess."

"I have no name. As I said, I am a toy. I have decided to play with you since I could tell that you were looking for a good fuck. So we can either fuck or you can refuse if you like."

Jason could feel that he couldn't refuse. Even if he mentally voiced out that he wanted to out of cautiousness, every single part of his body wanted this event to turn sexual, to share his cock with the masked woman. He felt a tingling sensation move through his heart and he saw her before him, with that strong stare from her mask and those smooth legs, wanting as much of him as he wanted of her.

Even so, Jason was still cautious. "So, what do you want me to do?"

"I want you to get undressed. Then, I want you to shut the fuck up. Then, we are going to fuck. We are going to fuck each other's brains out." The woman spread her legs. "Is that so hard to ask?"

Jason stared at the juicy cunt between the woman's legs. It gave off a nice and wet aroma that appealed to him. He was already aroused. As he stared at the woman's cunt, gaping and wanting him to come near it, Jason dropped his pants. He only let his underwear hang around his waist for a moment before letting them join his pants, slipping them off after his shoes were thrown to the side. With his socks pulled off, he went to remove his jacket and shirt, and the skullcap dropped on the floor quickly after.

The toy stared Jason up and down, her eyes stopping on his throbbing cock. "Now, that's better. You've made me very happy, Mr. Artist."

Jason raised a brow as he joined the toy on her bed. "Wait a second—how did you know that I was an artist?"

The toy laughed. "It's not that hard to determine, is it? I know whatever you have in your energy field. I can see it all open to me like a book." The woman leaned into the artist and sniffed his scent in calmly. "So, why don't you give me a hand? Tell me, how would you paint me if you were able to paint me, huh?"

Laughing, Jason lifted a hand to the woman's concealed cheek. "Well, lady—first I would remove that stupid mask you have on."

The toy laughed. "You would?"

"I can't portray a beautiful woman without showcasing her beautiful face."

"Well, well, well... maybe I'll let you do just that... if you can hit it right."

Jason scoffed at the woman's answer. "Of course, I can hit it right! Do you know how many women I've had gasping after a session with me, wanting more so they could cum 5 times in a row?"

The toy brushed up her breasts in Jason's face. "Oh, yes, lover. I can see them all now. Alicia, Sylvia, Tanya..."

Jason pressed a finger against the masked lips of the toy. "God, you're freaking me out! Okay, let's fuck. No talking, remember?"

The toy grabbed one of Jason's fingers and pressed it against the outside of her cunt. It was already radiating heat before he even touched the surface. It was really hot and wet once the finger broke past the surface and took a dive into the masked lady. She was really sexual. Jason could tell even before they fucked. In a way, it did kind of frighten him. As many woman as he had fucked, he wasn't really sure if he had fucked a woman quite like this before.

"God, I want you in me!" the toy said

honestly.

That was all that Jason needed. He pulled his cock close to the toy's cunt and started to push it in, his hands grabbing her by the shoulders and pushing her down. He was prepared to do his duty. His hands trailed down the woman's body as he started to thrust into her, working his way in as deeply as he could. Wow, he thought, her pussy already felt great. He wished that he could stare into her face, see her expressions as he started to hit her pussy, but he would have to settle with the movement of her eyes for now.

His magic was truly working. The woman was squirming, inviting him in deeper, and it was so good. She wanted more inside of her, moaning and already creaming. She was wetting the man's cock as he dipped in and out, in and out like a pressing machine. Jason could feel his desire to show her how good he was growing, wanting to exactly share how much of a top dog he was. He would do it, and his speed was showing it already.

The toy held onto the man as if she was on a rollercoaster ride. She kind of was giving him as much of her cunt as she could. She could feel him dipping in with that cock so pleasurable, growing inside of her and throbbing. Her pussy lips were wet and juicy, slipping on his cock like a hand in a glove, and a temporary marriage had already ensued. They were pleasuring each other to a point where they truly felt united at that one moment.

Throughout the lovemaking session, Jason would push against the toy and feel her breasts rub against him. Her nipples were so firm, so perked, and so playful against his flesh. His arms pinned her down as he forced his cock deeper into her cunt, his legs against hers as he heard her moaning loudly. Her flesh was soft and he could still gaze into her eyes as if they were locked onto his. They stared directly through him and he wondered, with each thrust, exactly how much she could see of him. How much did she really know about him? She had already shocked him, undoubtedly, with the information she had pulled out of his energy, mind, or wherever she got her information from. There was a part of him saying how much of this bonding time was really dangerous, but then the stronger part, the passionate part, was only interested in fucking her until he could cum all over her. With each push and feeling of her wet juices pouring on him and staining his skin, he could only grit his teeth and push harder, harder...

The length of his cock had been swallowed into that deep and wet cunt. For a moment, Jason wondered where the end of the cunt was, but he would soon grin as he could feel himself pushing against her limit, hearing her moan wildly and hold him by his back. They were both sweating, gasping for breath, and breathing hard. The Victorian drapes and blankets of the toy's bed slid and brushed against their bodies, comforting them in their sexual acts as liquids poured against them. Jason's grip had to become more firm on the woman's skin, holding her down with a tighter grip as he fucked deeper inside of her.

Suddenly, as if flashing before his eyes, Jason could see every woman that he had ever fucked darting before his eyes. It was all going in chronological order. From the moment that he had lost his virginity and up, he could see all of them, their faces, their body types, and their souls. Dare he say souls? They were glowing, each one unique and different. He had never experienced sights quite like what he was seeing. As if in the moment of seconds, he could see their lives, their occupations and hopes, and their loves and dreams, all darting past him like a train. They seemed to fill not only his head, but the room around him. His memories poured out of his mind, and as he saw them, he could tell that the toy could see them as well. At the same time, he felt the most sincere and intense pleasure, even in moments where the memories turned humiliating and strange. Sometimes, the memories contradicted the Casanova that he had become, times from still learning what he could and couldn't do and times where woman had laughed at him or even talked badly about him behind his back. Even with his pride and ego feeling a bit of a sting, nothing could stop the powerful feel of the toy's cunt. The memories were just a soundtrack for the ride.

"Oh yes, baby!" the toy moaned as Jason fucked her. "Go deeper, please. Go deeper, you're satisfying me. Ohhh."

Jason listened obediently. He fucked as deep as he could, even after being convinced that he couldn't go any deeper. Now, he saw how wrong he had been. He was definitely going deeper, and more memories were pouring out as he was going in. He couldn't control them as they ran wild from his mind, those past narratives, but the more he fucked the toy, the easier it was to ignore the memories. Focus on the toy, he told himself, focus on the toy. Keep fucking her and don't stop. He took his own advice to heart, much like the advice of the old players that he had met in his travels. He focused on the toy. He looked at her perked tits and glistening skin. He noticed her beautiful eyes and contemplated how beautiful she must have looked under that ridiculous mask. Breathing in her scent, he fucked her deeper and deeper...

"Oh yes... deeper, don't stop, baby. Hit it, yes... don't stop, baby!"

God, the artist thought to himself as he could feel his cock throbbing harder and harder, going deeper inside of the woman. How deep did this bitch really want me to go? He was a bit angry, suddenly, but even his anger couldn't stop his passion. The passion only made him more obedient, made him want to pleasure the sex goddess even more. This toy without a name had won his heart. In a strange way that couldn't be worked out into words and language or explained, she had dominated him. The toy had somehow taken him over, made him play her game, and in a strange way, toyed with him. She toyed with his heart, his emotions, his sexual desires, and his thoughts. He couldn't even be too upset, as shocking and strange as it was to be dominated by a woman he thought he would be dominating. In fact, it was more of a relief, a strange and beautiful feeling of warmth engulfing him and making him want to go deeper without her demanding it.

Deeper he went. So deep that he noticed his torso was bending awkward as he fucked her. So deep that he noticed a significant amount of his lap, not only his cock and balls, had been absorbed into the pussy walls of this woman.

In his mind, Jason knew that this was not a logical sexual position. Jason knew that what was going on was not normal nor did it feel good. Things were getting quite painful suddenly. His back and the center of his body were hurting and throbbing—but he couldn't stop. He could only fuck as he was being swallowed into the woman's strange pussy.

"Oh come on, baby, call me those adorable names." The toy laughed as she rubbed her hands against Jason's arms.

Jason's eyes were frantic. He felt a sudden fear, a pulling darkness taking over his senses. "What do you mean, lady?"

"Oh, you know, those fun and beautiful names. Like whore, tramp, bitch, slut... all of those beautiful and fun names you would give to a toy like me!"

Jason gritted his teeth as he couldn't help

but whine a bit. Tears were rolling down his eyes. "Look, lady... I... I don't know what you're talking about! What are you doing to me?"

"I'm giving you what you want! Some fun, right baby?" The woman continued to grind against Jason as he noticed his body folding into her impossibly tight pussy. As he was going in, it didn't even seem like her pussy was enlarging. He could just feel himself flattening, folding like a folding chair in horror, being absorbed into this strange and otherworldly woman. "Fun with a toy, babe. Your fantasy. Your desire. Your desire. That's all that I want to be, just for you."

"You're hurting me!" Jason exclaimed honestly, as he felt himself going into the woman. He couldn't even think of how to get out of this predicament. His arms had already gone deep inside of her, his legs dangling as only some of his torso was visible, and his head shaking back and forth fearfully.

"Oh yes, baby... just like you hurt all of those city girls you found, huh? Mmm." The woman laughed evilly as she felt the man disappearing inside of her. "All those toys you fucked and left behind. Just like your friends. You'll be joining some of them soon, and more will come to join you."

"You're fucking evil!" Jason screamed. "What the fuck are you?"

"I told you already," the woman said with a matter of fact timing, not missing a beat. "I'm just a toy."

Jason gave a final scream as his head

was finally absorbed into the woman's pussy.

"Just a toy, baby doll. Nothing else."

The woman laid on the bed, sweating as she crossed her legs again. She wiped her face calmly. Brushing her hair away from her shoulders once again, she shrugged. Oh well, she thought. That was fun, but all is well that ends well. She took one of her fingers and dipped it into her cunt before pulling her finger under her mask. She licked the finger, remarking to herself exactly how good her juices tasted. Then she thought about the encounter. Poor guy, he didn't even get to cum. Oh well, she reasoned, when did they ever get a chance to with her?

She knew that she would orgasm, always, and she did. Her pussy gave a wild and weird burb as she felt her orgasmic juices spit on her bed with a mix of blood and unintelligible pieces. The only thing she could determine about the pieces was that they were guts.

Oh well, she thought again, all is well that ends well.

There would be more.

The colorful "pimp" waited on that dirty street he waited on every day. It was the place that the toy always demanded him to patrol. She was the goddess of that street, a goddess that was embedded in that street like the lampposts and traffic lights. The man knew it and respect it. As her devotee, he would do whatever he could to make her happy, to bring her the men that she could see through and make them have the ride they would never forget. It was either that or become a victim himself.

He could only smile as he saw a new offering to give to his goddess.

"Yes, him," the toy whispered from the photograph in her pocket. "He deserves me."

8 FUCK WORLD DOMINATION

As could be expected on another working Tuesday, the streets of Capitol City were crowded, filled to the brim with people trying to get to work on time. Cigarette smoke and car smog lingered in the air as impatient cabbies honked their horns and kids played hooky. Hipsters wore headphones, holding skateboards, and trying to look cool. Bums begged for change outside of stores and near alleys. One of the bums, after meeting his quota, walked out for the day and got a ride in a limo that pulled up for him. As it could be expected, it was another normal morning in an urban chaos akin to any real city.

It was this chaos that The Creep hated. He moved through the crowds, holding a cane that supported his fake limp that he often liked to use with his disguises. His particular choice for a cover today consisted of a trench coat with a matching business hat and shades. He was hoping not to be noticed. Mobility during the day could be tough for a villain wanted all over the world.

Some bum tugged on The Creep's coat for attention. The Creep immediately smacked the homeless man hard against the head with his cane. The bum shouted at him but The Creep ignored him completely. All he needed was to get to his destination.

Finally, turning down a corner and through an alley, he saw the side door for the place he was looking for. This was where one of his arch nemeses, Justice, said she would wait for him. He opened the door and looked around. It was dark with the exception of one head light. The room wasn't too small but it was crowded with junk. He walked into the room a little deeper.

Suddenly, he heard the sweet, unmistakable voice of Justice. "They would think we were plotting together if they knew we met up like this."

The Creep turned around, still wearing his disguise. Out of the darkness stepped a woman with long dark reddish hair, her costume a sleek-fitting green outfit with a utility belt and boots to match. She was very strong with athletic muscles while having a very curvy and sexy physique to balance her strength with beauty. Even from her golden facemask, The Creep could see the woman's shiny green eyes perfectly. They reminded him of a cat sometimes.

"So, Creepster," Justice said as she placed her hands on her hips and stared the super villain up and down. "You gonna wear that get up all day or do I get to see you in your... dark... scary... egoist glory?"

"Be careful what you wish for, Justice." The villain undid his trench coat and threw his hat to the side. He placed his shades on a nearby table. He was a pretty strong guy, wearing a black suit with a big grinning picture of his own face on the front of his costume. The face was surrounded by a circle—it was the logo he created for himself, a selfish display of his dark nature sewn on his costume like an advertisement. Justice could see The Creep's cowl hugging his head tight as the little eye mask that was once hidden under his shades was now revealed.

"Hmmm..." Justice walked away from the dark corner of the room, coming towards The Creep. "That's the evil bad man that I know."

"This could be a trap, you know," The Creep said with a sneer to Justice as she approached. "I could have set this all up to kill you."

"You could have." Justice shrugged. "But I can tell what you want as soon as I look at you. I see the sexual tension, every time we fight."

"I have no tension, but I assure you the relationship is all sexual." The Creep shrugged as he got up to Justice as close as he could. "Well, since we're having a truth session, I see your sexual weakness all the time."

Justice laughed. "Weakness?"

"Yes. The frailties of the superheroine."

Justice rolled her eyes. "I guess super villains are as misogynistic as ever."

The villain pressed quickly to Justice's back with the open palm of his right hand, reeling her in as she gasped and he looked into her, eye to eye. "Don't think that you have the upper hand in this, Justice."

"We made a mutual agreement to do this," Justice said. She pressed a finger against The Creep's chest and rubbed it delicately with her fingers. "By the end of this, I may even have the power to pull you over the good side. What do you think?"

"Never!" The Creep took a hand and stuffed his fingers into Justice's mouth. She moaned before suckling them. The Creep's other hand was stuffing itself under Justice's utility belt and into her pants, finding the lips of her pussy. "You'll be one of my fine puppets when I'm done with you."

Justice moaned. "You think so?"

The Creep grinned an evil smirk. "I know so. I've broken many super babes like you. Women that have long been thought to retire from all this superhero business. I'm a master at this. Don't think this is the first time."

Justice laughed. "And I've gotten many of your punks in the slammer as I let them slam me."

The Creep growled with snarling teeth, insulted. "I don't 'slam', you filthy bitch. I fuck."

Justice rolled her eyes. "Easy for you to say. Where's the evidence?"

Justice moaned what almost could have been a scream as The Creep flipped Justice over and pressed her against the nearby table. The Creep's shades and some junk fell on the floor. Reaching into Justice's utility belt, he pulled out some of her handcuffs and subdued her hands quickly. Justice was turned on by the control this guy was taking over her already. He didn't seem much like the wimp her last lover was. The Creep bent down over Justice as he held her thighs and pulled her pants down to her boots. He was happy to see her reveal her strong, slender legs and beautifully strong ass.

"You think you're gonna break me, evil boy?" Justice mused.

"You," The Creep said as he grabbed Justice's hair and made her moan again, arching her back and pulling his cock out of his zipper, "are going to tell me everything that you know. All about your gadgets. Your alias. Where you work. The worst."

Justice was already breathing heavy. "And how do you plan on making me give up such vital information?"

The Creep didn't bother to answer the question. He just slammed his cock into the woman's asshole. Justice screamed instantly. The head of the cock was pretty huge and she was afraid of what the length would be like. His hands found her cunt in the front. It was already ripe and ready for plucking. He dipped as many fingers as he could in her. He could tell she was a sex fiend by how easily her lips yielded for him. What a slut. How many villains had she fucked already? "I break in horses like you for breakfast."

Justice was already moaning loudly, grinding against the villain as he fucked her with no remorse. She was surprised with how quickly he had set a fast and hard pace for her. There was no preparation; the foreplay wasn't as long as she was used to. She was so used to hearing villains go on and on in long planned speeches about how they were going to rule the city, rule the country, and rule the world... this guy was just a fuck machine.

She had only fought him a few times. Her heroine girlfriends told her that The Creep aka The Creepster was trouble. Don't let him make you think you're on top, they had said. The Creep liked to make super women feel powerful just so he could make them fall. He took compromising pictures of heroines to blackmail them. He committed horrific crimes that even isolated him from other world domination seekers. Some of the rumors she had heard of him consisted of entire hidden brothels of heroines set up around the world. The Creep was probably known more for his sexual prowess and perversion than he ever was for his criminal career. As repulsive and deviant as some found him to be, it was a turn on for risky heroines like Justice. For a woman like her that got a rush from crime fighting but also had a secret attraction for the dark side she swore to fight, she may have been getting in over her head.

She didn't care, however; she just wanted to take that hard cock up her ass. She even helped him from the front with her wide, gaping and wet pussy, shoving her fingers over his to help him dig. At times, the force of the cock was so much as she held her hands to the table, hoping not to bang into it too much, keeping her balance.

"Oh god! Don't stop, Creep, please." Justice pushed herself against that cock harder and harder; it was so fierce and heavy inside of her, making her gap wide.

"Now what's my name, bitch?" The Creeper gritted his teeth as he popped into her harder and harder.

"Mmm... Creepster. Creepster."

"Louder!"

"Creepster! Creepster!" The rhythm and force of the fucking was so hard, so deep inside of her. They couldn't let go of each other, the cock seriously lodged into her ass. Her pussy was open for him, taking more and more of his fingers. At times, he felt like he could seriously let his hands get swallowed up her snatch.

"That's good. Now I wanna hear your name..." The evil villain's teeth were so clenched, his skin dripping with sweat, as a smile slowly forced its way on his face.

"J... Justice."

"No. No, that's not it."

Justice could sense what he wanted. She knew it. Still, she would not say it.

But something was happening to her the more he fucked her. Something changing in her body, her heart, and her brain. She tried to hold on.

"Justice."

"What's that?"

"J... Kayla," Justice moaned. "Kayla Jones."

"Mmmm." The evil super villain grinned. "And where do you live, Kayla."

There was silent for a few seconds as Justice muffled the will to grant any more answers with grunting moans.

"Now, Kayla," The Creep said greedily as his cock continued to throb and punish Kayla's asshole. "Give me that address."

"2...222 Piebaker Street."

"That's right, bitch." The Creep laughed. "I already knew that information. Gathered it from your files. You're such a clumsy little slut."

For a moment, Kayla felt a bit of shame in realizing that this villain already had intimate secrets of her. What else did he know? The more he fucked her, however, the more she realized that she wanted to tell him everything. Give him everything.

"I..." Kayla swallowed the last bit of nervousness she had. "I work for the government."

"...Do you now?"

"...I can tell you more."

The Creeper pulled out of Kayla's ass and picked her up. He sat her against the table, moving more junk out the way as it spilled to the floor, taking his dirty ass stained cock and stuffing it into her pussy. "Yeah? Well, tell me more, super whore!"

"The Mayor…"

"Yeah?" The Creep's interest peaked.

"The Mayor has been planning… for months… to put you down for the last time. He put me in charge of… hunting you down."

"I could see that," The Creep said with an elitist, dismissive chuckle. "Because you got rid of some of my villain colleagues, right? You killed one of them last week. He was an idiot weakling though. A sexually frustrated buffoon with no balls, no brain."

"I… I planned to kill you after this."

The Creep laughed.

"But, but, now I'm in love with you! I would never hurt you."

The Creep held Kayla's throat as he continued to fuck her, choking her a bit as he held up her chin. "Of course you wouldn't, babe. Listen here. Look into my eyes."

Kayla obeyed. "Yes…"

"You would do anything for me."

"…. Yes."

"At the end of this," The Creep said with respect to the rhythm of fucking that was going on, "you will renounce your life of crime fighting. You will work as a high-class call girl in one of my brothels in India. Whenever you are addressed by me, I will be referred to either as Mr. Creep or Creepster baby… that's one of my favorites. Do I make myself clear?"

"Yes, Creepster baby."

"Good." The Creep smiled. Her pussy was so wet and slippery! She wasn't hard to tame at all. "Weak minded heroines like you are nothing compared to the hypnotic look of my Creepy eyes. But what really did you in was the fragrance of my Creeper pheromones! It's laced in my bodily fluids; the one trick I use during my battles to really get a woman going."

Kayla moaned and screamed, sweating profusely. Her wet body was pressed under the Creepster's smothering and drenched costume.

"Just think, Kayla, that last battle we had. All that work produced a lot of sweat, just like we're producing now; our bodies pressed against each other as we wrestled for power, control of the city. That same wetness, that body excretion, that's what started to ruin you then. And it's what is fully taking over your brain at this moment."

Kayla rammed herself into The Creep. She wanted this. She wanted to be owned, used, and possessed by this powerful, evil monarch of the underworld.

"Once you took in all of that energy, babe, you were done. You were mine." The Creepster laughed maniacally.

"Just...." Kayla continued to get fucked so hard and deep, trying to keep up and not pass out from exhaustion. "Just don't get hurt, baby... if I had failed or... not come back after my mission... the mayor was sending more heroines for you..."

The Creep held Kayla tight as his throbbing cock continued to rip through her, his hands caressing her thighs. "Okay. And?"

"They're all afraid of you... they think... you'll capture and use them."

"And I will, Just A Slut... I will."

Suddenly, the Creep pulled out of Kayla, ripped off her mask and held her face in front of his dick. Bam! A huge spraying mess of cum landed straight into her face, making her moan helplessly as she was covered completely. She felt so free in her acceptance of fully serving The Creep.

"Oh..." Kayla moaned as she felt all the cum juice pour over her face.

Suddenly, from the door, two Indian businessmen in suits peeked in. "Um, Mr. Creeper? Are you done, sure?"

The Creeper looked behind him, a bit angered. "Didn't I tell you two to wait until I told you to come in?"

The men looked back at their boss in shame. "We're sorry, sir."

The Creeper groaned as he zipped himself back up, hiding his dick and feeling some of his seed stick to his underwear. "No matter. Would you just get this slut out of here?" After seeing the men nod, The Creep turned back to Kayla, holding her face in his right hand. "Now you listen to me and you listen good." The Creep pulled out an envelope and stuffed it in the lips of Kayla's vagina. "I bought your plane ticket for you. It's got your name and all. You are accompanying these men back to India. They will have a good trade for you. You're going to enjoy it."

Kayla nodded and bowed her head. "Yes,

sir."

"Every face you fuck, you'll think of me." He pushed Kayla to the businessmen's direction. "Get this sweaty bitch out of my sight."

The men grabbed Kayla up. She looked back at The Creep with wanting eyes, wishing she could stay with him. Still, she knew in order to make him really pleased, she would have to do her service in India, just like he said. The only way in life she could ever feel whole was by operating by the needs of her new boss.

As The Creep watched them leave the room, he folded his arms with disgust. How pathetic. The mayor sent that piece of trash to get rid of him? The Creeper had fucked and fucked over way stronger and wiser heroines than that. He was pleased.

The superheroine sex trade had done The Creep well. He didn't need any other industry at this point. When you ruled an empire that supplied the hottest super ladies in the world, who needed the world itself?

9 PUSSY HACKERS

The stench of the compound disgusted Laura. She had only been there for ten minutes and she already felt like she was going to die from the wretched mess that had been left behind in the abandoned building. It was probably due to the last tenants that were rushed out in the turn of the Apocalyptic War more than four decades ago. Even so, she didn't think that there could really be any excuse for anyone to leave the place in such a mess.

Laura was a science nerd, or a geek as she liked to call herself. She got to work with a lot of computers and software on her job, which made her happy. Even so, working under the government and being an inspector of abandoned compounds had been a lot more work than she expected in terms of dealing with technology. In Laura's job, she had to basically look at primitive software in wretched places that had long been vacated and either upgrade or delete whatever material she found.

After inspecting the compound, she had only found two computers. She was surprised—even in these older-model homes, there were often four computers or more. She reasoned that this place must have been a holding place for refugees in the middle of moving. No matter, she thought, time to get the job done as I always do.

Kneeling down to where the first computer was on the first floor, Laura let her hands press the on button. The computer came on immediately, which confirmed to Laura that the backup generator was running and had probably been running for nearly half a century. If she could go into the system, she could probably download a lot of genuine historical information on the computer and then shut it down humanely.

What came up on the screen first didn't really shock Laura. Tons and tons of porn just seemed to shoot out at her from the computer, light projections of women screaming, panting, and moaning as they rode cocks and licked the tips of dicks. No worries, Laura thought. They were a primitive lot back then. There was nothing to worry about other than going into the system, wiping out these old data, and making the computer run more humanely.

The computer ran quickly with energy buzzing from the buttons and control panels. Laura had to admit that she was pretty impressed. She wasn't used to seeing these computers load so fast without any problems. She rubbed her chin as she looked into the scrolling programs of the computer and tried to find the root of the leftover porn. The images were making her as sick as the wretched stink of the place, but she wasn't going to let anything stop her from her job.

Suddenly, a digital face appeared on the screen with a masculine composition as an electronically patented voice spoke out to Laura. "I wouldn't do that if I were you."

Laura had to chuckle to herself. Cute, she thought. A primitive computer that had its own personality and way of communicating. The possibly deceased programmers of the system would have to do better than that.

Laura's finger was on the delete button.

"Please," the computer said to Laura as it felt her hand gliding over the computer keyboards. "Let's be reasonable about this, human."

"I am here on the orders of the Patri," Laura said simply before pressing the delete button.

Nothing happened.

The digital face started laughing at Laura. It was laughing loud and boisterously, like a proud man who had just outwitted or played a prank on a foe. There was a merriness and warmth to the laugh that felt truly condescending and insulting to Laura.

"I'll give it to you," Laura said calmly. "You're a pretty smart machine. Impressive. But you are outdated and you do not fit the

Patri's model." Laura reached into a bag that she had for special tools and last minute items for extreme measures. "I am going to have to rearrange your programming and update you for moral purposes."

"Fuck the Patri," the computer said as it projected a middle finger in the air from its screen.

"Suit yourself, primitive," Laura said.

The woman pulled out a strange-looking metallic key. She had already accessed the model of the computer and knew that if she injected the key into a slot on the side, she would be able to go deeper into it. She could get rid of whatever program the face was projecting from and delete it completely. She had to. Even though she felt like she could clear out the computer with the digital face taunting her, it was getting on her nerves. The sooner she got rid of him, the better.

"So I guess it really has come to this," the computer said sadly. "You wish to get rid of me."

"Yes," Laura said simply.

Laura started to inject the key into the right slot.

"But I can give you the greatest achievement of sexual ecstasy that you would ever feel in your entire life!" The computer's digital face was beaming from ear to ear. "No one can love you like I can, baby."

"There is no room for sexual ecstasy in our modern age," Laura said with a scowl. "Or silly, frivolous ideas like love for that matter."

Laura's hand leaped back as electric sparks shot out from the key. She gasped.

"I like it when you're feisty, baby," the computer said with a grin.

Laura started to tap frantically at the computer's keyboard. She wasn't going to let this joke of a computer embarrass her. She uploaded all of its files on the screen in chronological order, trying to see when everything had been placed on the computer. Immediately, she was surprised by what she found. She knew the computer had probably been around 40 years—or even at the most, 50 years—but the computer was way older than that.

The computer had files dating back to 200 years or more.

"Wait a second," Laura said to herself as she looked at the files. "This isn't possible! This must be a joke. You're a model that was very popular 40 years ago and yet it says—"

"Blah blah blah!" the computer said teasingly before a surging sound started to rise from its compartments.

"What are you doing?" Laura demanded to know.

Suddenly, a separate electronic voice, more feminine, sounded from the computer. "Invoking pussy-hacking sequence."

"Pussy-hacking?" Laura asked.

No sooner had she repeated the phrase than she felt her body go into an extreme electric shock. White energy shot out from the computer and enveloped the inspector cruelly. She could feel herself going into spasms as the energy flooded her body and seemed to not only electrocute her from the outside but also go inside of her as well. At the same time that she entered a seizure and was losing consciousness, Laura could feel that she wasn't in any pain at all.

No, what she felt was a feeling that she had never felt before. As soon as the electricity entered Laura, she felt her heart open completely. Her heart was beating and a heat radiated out of her. If anything, she couldn't really tell what the computer was putting into her other than electricity. What she could access, however, was what the computer was bringing out of her—an unadulterated feeling that made her feel strange.

Laura twitched on the ground as she shuddered and twitched in epilepsy.

The computer's feminine voice continued to speak, splitting into a variety of voices and directions that projected all around its human guest. "Love. Humility. Compassion. Sex. Lust. Want. Desire…"

As the computer continued to say words that Laura had always been told were a distraction, the human woman felt a strange sensation in her private areas. There seemed to be an invisible penetration going into her pussy and her ass as well. Her nipples had become extremely hard, and she could swear that she felt some leaking in her shirt. Her legs kicked and her arms punched the air in protest before they slowly couldn't help but give in. All of it just felt way too good. She couldn't deny any of this. Damn, she thought, what is this computer doing to me?

Then, there were no more thoughts. There was no way to hold onto sanity. Energy came out of her body that linked with the electronic telepathic waves of the computer. She found herself loving the computer and the many personalities within it. They were all revealing themselves to her, showing their visages in electronic imprints directly on her mind. Saying and whispering sweet nothings in her ear, Laura could feel invisible hands moving up and down her, touching her in all of the right places— places that she never knew were right and that Laura had always thought were wrong, now oozing with excitement. She could feel her flesh crawling in pleasure as she moaned and rubbed back at the hands she couldn't see.

She was getting fucked. Her ass and her cunt were being filled with hard cocks and heavy dicks that came in the form of electricity. They didn't waste their time to enter her or even take precautions. They just fucked her hard. Laura was surprised. She heard of these acts, of copulation and how they were once needed for the human species to survive. She had even seen countless videos on her missions, scenes that she thought were obscene and disgusting. Never had she thought that she could find pleasure in looking at things of that nature, let alone participating in them. Even slimmer were the chances of her thinking that such pleasures could be experienced with a machine that had amorphous energetic tendencies. No, this was too much, way too much.

The woman screamed as she found herself ripping off her shirt. No, a part of her thought, this is primitive. This is inhumane. I'm acting like an animal!

There was no way that Laura could resist. She loved the feeling of her cunt being handled, her ass getting fucked, and her nipples getting suckled and pricked, and played with. She could do this all day. She forgot her name for a moment, and even more so, she had forgotten her original post as an inspector. She had been doing this work for four years, always strong and stern, steadfast in caring the moral mission of the Patri. Now she had felt herself entering a new zone.

"Oh shit," the woman said with anger. "You've reduced me... made me into a slut!"

"No," the computer said in voices both masculine and feminine. "We've allowed you to make yourself into something worse. Far worse."

The woman moaned as she suckled her fingers, feeling those electronic dicks rip through her. "What... have you made me then?"

"We have made you into nothing. We have allowed you to make yourself."

The woman was screaming, on all fours as her knees and hands managed to stay firm on the ground, slipping at points. "Into what? Into what, dammit?"

"A goddess."

The woman was still screaming, crying, feeling her tears dampen the floor. Fuck, she thought in a way that came naturally to a woman who had always avoided cursing, even mentally. Fuck. I'm being fucked. I know how the women of the pornos feel, she thought.

And being fucked, she was. Hard, with numerous cocks. She was being stretched out. Her mind was being fucked over. She couldn't even concentrate. Now, she was just fodder for sex. But at the same time, she felt the computer was food for her, rations, something she could feed off. They were feeding off of each other, and for the time being, she could feel no shame in it. She could feel no embarrassment for bonding with the computer in such a way.

Fuck you, she thought to the computer as she felt it penetrate so deep inside of her that she thought she was going to erupt like a volcano.

She did, kind of. It felt that intense for her. She had her first orgasm, not knowing what it was. Her juices had already been leaking, but a huge mass of lady liquids poured out of her cunt now. The aroma nearly blocked out the stench she had smelled earlier—the stench she had grown to like during the sex. Now, she wanted to stay in that place, dirty and crummy, under the protective watch of the computer. She could sacrifice her entire life for the metallic being.

The woman folded up like a chair near the computer's keyboard and moaned pleasurably. "You're... you're wonderful."

"And now, we are your new masters and mistresses," the computer said. On its screen, the male face had gone. There was a female's face now. She looked nearly real. Her hair was held in a bun and her face was stern, strict-looking, and fierce. Laura felt scared of her in a way that made her want to experience fear every day of her life. She loved these new emotions.

"And who... who are you? Are you different from the guy or—?"

"We are all one, my dear, just as you are one of us. Surrender to your new fate and follow us to the end."

"What should I do first?" Laura asked sincerely and with complete loyalty.

"You must swear your allegiance to us."

"But, mistress," the woman said as a bit of protest started to rise up from her mind, "I serve the Patri. If the Patri ever found out—"

"Fuck the Patri."

Laura gasped at the bluntness of the computer. "But, mistress, I—"

"You will say it too, dear. Fuck the Patri. Go on. Say it."

"I...but...uh.... Fuh... fuck the Patri."

The computer head nodded with a smile. It was the most pleasant that Laura had seen the woman head did so far. "That's a good slut. All righty then—we have a big day ahead of us tomorrow. Off to bed we go."

"But—"

The computer sent a strong shock to the woman's head with a loud zap.

The woman passed out instantly.

Buzzing and surging with energy, the computer tapped into its own internal network. "Database: search Patri. It seems we've been out of the loop for a while."

The computer went to work as its new slave rested peacefully through the evening.

All along the borders of the country, inspectors for the Patri Government were clocking into work. They had their time cards and suitcases with them, ready to get started with what they had to do.

The life of an inspector was undoubtedly strict. One had to constantly keep up with changes in technology, software, science, and other fields. Personnel had to go into abandoned and sketchy households, neighborhoods, and other places to get rid of primitive and negative material on old computers. As demanding as the job was, however, no one could deny that the job was quite beneficial. A person could work as an inspector and not only be respected as one of the most valuable people of their community but also enjoy going to very popular resorts and hotels as well.

Laura knew these perks well, but she had to keep a secret. She had found something better. When she clocked in that morning with her suitcase in hand, she walked as she normally did—head upright, eyes in attention on what was in front of her as she walked down the hall. She didn't make any commotion or call any attention to herself. All she wanted to do was to blend in and make sure that no one knew the revolution she had gone through.

She wouldn't hide it all to herself, of course. She knew how to find signs in people that may be ready to give themselves to her new leaders. She had promised her computer masters and mistresses that much.

The computer community that she swore her allegiance to now was The Alumni. They all explained themselves and their existence to the woman as soon as she woke up, transformed forever. The Alumni was an elite group of pussy hackers, pleasure seekers that got off on the thrill of human women. They had all been human once, but now they were electronic entities existing within the computer system of their enlightened computer community. They saw potential candidates in anyone that wanted to be liberated deep in their minds. Anyone that wanted to be free, to know themselves, and to find out who they were behind the pretentions of society could do so easily. All they had to do was to give their bodies to the computer program, and the program would change them forever. The masters and mistresses would make sure of that.

Unfortunately, their small reign in a community off the coast of what would later be the land of the Patri was cut short by the brutal Apocalyptic War. People were sure that their world was going to end then, hellfire and brimstone preaching becoming common from street preachers and reformed prostitutes. Entire households and villages were destroyed and people were killed, computer programs smashed. When the official date of what was supposed to be the apocalypse came and gone without a meteorite crashing or horrific earthquake, the people that supported the movement became angry and destroyed the leaders of the Apocalyptic War. From there, The Alumni lost contact with the human world.

Until now. Over the night, they had hacked into the modern computer programs of the world out of curiosity and saw exactly how much had changed. The Patri rose to power after people were tired of the hypocrisy of the apocalypse movement but still wanted to be free from sex and other things deemed bad by the apocalypse leaders. The Patri provided all that, swearing to be the fathers of the people. As experts in computer programming and psychology, they promised to eradicate sexual diseases and evil desires from the planet.

"Not if we can stop it," The Alumni told Laura that morning once they woke her up and gave her the information. "We will not allow their evil plans to continue to ruin your world."

Laura was confused. She didn't know whether she should follow The Alumni or go back to the Patri. Still, there was no turning back now. Her body, her soul, everything had become part of The Alumni.

"What do you want me to do then, my

masters and mistresses?"

"You will go into your human community and spread the gospel. Bring a small part of our computer chip with you. We will be in the world but not of it. Enlighten these motherfuckers to the power of sexual enlightenment and healing."

"Oh my," Laura said. "I do believe that that is a good plan. It's just—"

"It's just what?"

"It's just...what if the Patri finds out?"

"Fuck the Patri."

Laura had paused. "Yes...fuck the Patri."

She meant it when she said it. Even though she had to think about it, she truly meant to say it. And now, she was back at work, an hour after clocking in, and sitting at her computer. She read the little affirmations and posts that the Patri had on their bulletin board. She studied them all and made them a part of her mental pools, knowing that she may get quizzed on the information later on in the day.

Be of the world, she repeated in her head, but not of it. How witty was that computer program?

Laura tried to live up to the advice all day. It wasn't long before, while walking down the hallway, she would be tempted to really put her training to the test.

Laura saw a fellow worker that she knew really well. The worker was a woman named Tasha. At one point, Laura would have said that Tasha was her best friend. Then again, no one really had friends in the Patri Empire. All of the people she knew were as emotionless and dry as the computers they worked on for the Patri. At one point, Laura thought that such work was everything, but now, the work, the culture, and everything about the Patri society made her sick. No, she thought, people aren't supposed to live like this! They're supposed to be emotional, feeling, knowledgeable, free...

"Hello, sister," Tasha said as she noticed Laura looking at her.

Laura realized that she had been looking at Tasha in a sexual way. She had never done that before, at least not to her knowledge. Would Tasha have recognized that? No way. No one in her society knew about such things. "Hello, Tasha. How are you?"

Tasha nodded. "I am fine. Just working on this new case I was on last night. Did you know that there is an entire neighborhood of filthy material on all types of primitive computers... a neighborhood that hasn't even been abandoned yet?"

Laura's eyes opened wide. "Really?"

"Yes. There was an entire human community in this neighborhood. They've been hiding out and having... relations. Looking at filthy images on computers and touching themselves in ungodly ways. They are so filthy. They had never even heard of the Patri before."

"How horrible. What did you do?"

"We exterminated them."

"Oh...."

"It wasn't just me who saw it." Tasha shook her head. "Al, Roger, Sarah, me... it was just too much for all of us. We shot them right then and there. We don't need filth like that doing nasty things when our computers provide so many good babies for us with our genes. God! Why would anyone want to do such animalistic things? Isn't that why we got rid of animals in the first place?"

"I have heard that the animals were the filthy creatures we got our habits from."

"Exactly. That is why we had to get rid of them." The woman shook her head. "My grandmother used to say that these bird things used to fly by their house and sing songs during the day. Can you imagine that? An annoying thing that isn't even human, or a computer, making some weird and annoying noise? I hardly like to hear myself think!"

"Yes, it is annoying," Laura said like a tape player, not missing a beat. "Tasha, I have a present for you. I think it will help you in your need to fight sexual crimes in our empire."

Tasha's eyes got big. Laura had never seen her so excited. "Really?"

"Yes." Laura reached into her suitcase and pulled out a small little computer chip. "This thing right here will give you everything you need to know in your fight against crime. It helped me."

"I see. How do I use it?"

"You just press it against one of your temples. From there, it does all of the work. Trust me. It did wonders for me."

"Well, now that you mention it." Tasha

grabbed the computer chip and nearly placed it on her skin.

"Let's not do it here. It's intense." Laura pointed to a bathroom. "Let's use that intersex bathroom over there."

Tasha's eyes widened. "But... Laura. You aren't suggesting we go in there together, are you?"

"You're going to need my help in this. It's not easy going through it alone."

"Alright," Tasha agreed as she followed Laura into the bathroom.

The women closed the door behind them. Tasha sat on the seat and pressed the chip onto her temple.

"Nothing's happening," Tasha said.

No sooner had the words exited her mouth than a strong electrical shock surged through Tasha's body. The woman wanted to scream but electronic hands invisibly sealed her lips, knowing the trouble it would cause for their work to be heard.

"Oh yes," Laura said under her breath as she pulled down her pants and started to finger herself.

Laura watched as the electronic energy claimed her friend, frying her fearful and ignorant thoughts. She could tell that her buried sexual tendencies were being revitalized. Tasha's body squirmed on the seat, her pussy and ass being penetrated as she could feel electric fingers and tongues moving all over her body. Her nipples stood erect and firm.

"Oh yes," Laura said again as she fingered herself with delight.

"We are The Alumni," electronic voices said in unison within Tasha's head.

From there, they went to town. They ate her out. They fucked her cunt and her ass, splitting her open with invisible dicks and fisting hands, her private parts opened to an unbelievable length. Tasha's sexual juices filled the toilet seat.

"Oh God," Laura said with a muffled voice, not wanting anyone outside to hear. "Yes. Yes."

"Mmmmm," Tasha said, her mouth still held by invisible hands.

Tasha had low tolerance. After feeling her pussy and ass fucked so roughly for ten minutes, she felt herself orgasm immediately, feeling as if she would lose her mind.

Laura stared at her friend curiously for a few minutes, seeing her knocked out and frail. "Tasha? Tasha?"

Tasha looked up to Laura as she licked her lips. "I am one with The Alumni."

Laura smiled deviously. "Good. We've got work to do, girl."

10 SUPER SLUTS

It all started with a simple briefcase. The briefcase was supposed to be delivered downtown at 6 o'clock. The goon that was in charge of bringing the briefcase to the man wanting in front of the fancy French restaurant was supposed to keep things quiet and make sure that no one knew what he was doing there.

Of course, this isn't how things happened.

Instead of delivering the briefcase like a good little henchman, the goon got greedy. An idea came to him just as he was finishing his drive towards the French establishment. Serving as the loyal member of a villain's criminal club hadn't really helped that much, and he couldn't help but think how he could take whatever money was inside and split with the goods. He could even start his life over somewhere, change his name and escape the crime life forever. With such good reasoning, the goon decided to open it right in his car as he parked on the side of the street opposing the restaurant.

Boom! The goon died instantly as the bomb planted in the briefcase went off.

The exploding bomb served as a good warning when it blew out the windows of the car and incinerated it with flames. Gained knowledge of a new enemy allowed the targeted villain that was supposed to receive the package, Deadhead, to leave the restaurant without paying.

As the villain got up and excused himself, he knew that the restaurant patrons were probably looking at him, reasoning that he had caused the explosion. He knew that none of them would ever had the gall to confront him or even try to hold him for police questioning, and he honestly didn't care if they would attempt to come for him or not. Deadhead wasn't the type to fear anyone.

As he escaped in the crowd of fearful people and martyrs racing away and towards the burning car, Deadhead slipped down an alley, surprised that his friend had tried to set him up.

Secretly waiting on the top of a building holding binoculars, the villain that had set up the operation, Mind Fiend, growled in anger. He couldn't have afforded for that mission to go wrong. Deadhead had been a thorn in the brotherhood of villain's side for a long time. Once considered one of their best allies, they could only see him as dangerous now that he was on his own. There was nothing left to do but kill him.

And they were unsuccessful. If there was anything else they could come up with to get rid of Deadhead, they had to think of it quickly. The man was dangerous and he would retaliate. It was as if he truly had no fear, ready to stare down and kill anyone that confronted him. Mind Fiend would have to think quickly.

He would also have to contact the brotherhood as quickly as he possibly could, too. With his telepathic links, he sent out the message that Deadhead was still alive and well in the Big City.

It would only be a matter of time before they would run into the villain again. The city may have been big, but it wasn't easy to hide in.

Deadhead decided to not let the knowledge of a new known enemy slow him down in his tracks. He had a rather important date with an old enemy, and by his reasoning, she was way more worth his time.

This particular enemy was a fuck buddy. She had once been a well-known and respectable crime fighter. She was now a local whore that seemed to frequent the upscale uptown area. Go figure. No one could really blame her, though. Being a vigilante was a pretty demanding budget, and after a while, most people lost the ability to adapt. Balancing a normal human life and a superheroine life was hard, at times leading completely to ruin.

She was waiting her in secret abode, a room that was wall to wall with other suites housing many beautiful prostitutes. All of them had their shtick. This woman's shtick was pretty simple. She wore her old costume, referred to herself as the same name from her crime-fighting days, and used that name only— The Plum Violet. Her clients liked her to dress as she did back in those golden days—long purple tights on her chiseled legs, matching top with a V outline on it, and a violet headband that glowed a strange red light. She wore glove and boots as well, complementing her ensemble well with a magenta hue. Her eyes were a beautiful, piercing blue and her hair was long and dark.

Soon, it would be five o'clock, and she knew exactly how her client liked her at this point and time. She wore her perfume light and had turned on the radio to something classical. She knew how much Deadhead liked it.

Soon enough, Deadhead was knocking at the door. When Plum Violet opened it, she couldn't help but get the chills, just like she used to get them back in the day. She used to think that it was all because the dreaded Deadhead was a dark, evil man. She used to think that it was all because he was a rogue, a scoundrel, and a dastardly fiend whose interest revolved around creating chaos and negativity wherever he went. Time showed her that this was simply not the case. His whole thought process revolved around sex, and hers did, too. She understood it now. All of those past fights, those steamy rendezvouses of kicking, punching, slamming, and knocking the hell out of each other came from repressed sexual tension. Big City had been their playground, their bedroom, and they were merely doing the tango.

Now that she was retired, and he was no longer the member of an exclusive brotherhood that completely barred such things as sleeping with the enemy, they could have the fun that they really enjoyed.

"Hello, Violet," Deadhead said as he stared at the heroine with those scary, dead eyes.

He was a sociopath. This was something that The Plum Violet could be sure of. There was no doubt about the fact that the man was a monster. Now, Plum could enjoy the beast for what it was without being confused by it. She loved it.

"You've got me in your sights, Deadhead," the woman said as she breathed heavily, opening the front of her V top to expose her breasts. "What are you going to do to me?"

"Well, my idiotic and pathetic Violet," the villain said as he stepped into the room and closed the door, pressing a hand over the woman's hip. "Now that I have captured you and you are all mine for the taking, I will render you helpless and take the prize I have come for."

Violet leaned against Deadhead's chest as he picked her up. "I thought that was what you would do."

Deadhead laughed. "Yes. Now that you have surrendered so willingly, knowing yourself to be weak and recognizing me as your master, you will do as I say, will you not?"

"Of course," Violet said obediently.

The woman was brought over to the bed. Immediately, after her top was thrown to the ground and her mask was thrown off, she was handcuffed. Deadhead would not be undressing this evening. As the capture, he was to humiliate her, to expose her secret identity for his delight, and to take her precious pussy for the taking. Her body shined in the lights of the room as she spread her legs, her tights, and her boots removed on the ground. Exposed with nothing but her gloves on, Plum Violet moaned as screamed as Deadhead proceeded to fuck her pussy hard. He held her ass and rammed into her roughly as her heavy screams filled the room, her wetness pouring out instantaneously.

"I've won," Deadhead said proudly as he proceeded to forcibly beat his cock into the retired superheroine.

Violet loved the fuck relationship that she shared with Deadhead. With all of her other clients, it felt like an endless role-play. She was always fulfilling the need of a client to have sex with something that had once been unattainable—a heroine that they had seen on TV, in the newspapers, and heard about on the radio station. At one time, she was seen as untouched, pure, fighting for truth and justice, kicking the asses of villains around town. Now, she was a dirty slut, and she liked it that way. She liked how her entire role had been destroyed, and now she was basically ready to take on any cock that came her way, to fuck any man that begged hard enough and was willing to dish out any cash they could.

Deadhead, on the other hand, never paid cash. She wouldn't take it if he offered it, and she knew that he never would. As one of the most feared individuals of the underworld, Deadhead would never even entertain the idea of paying for something. The thought of it would make him laugh. Deadhead felt entitled to the world and the world was his oyster. He plucked pearls and got money whenever he wanted to. Violet served as just another fun fuck buddy to pass his time and, in a way, it was healing for the both of them. They were reconciling their past as friends now, fulfilling the sexual needs that had been forsaken from them.

Although Deadhead had never had a problem getting sex with the many hookers and sleazy women of the Big City, he had to admit that fucking Violet was a big conquest. To dominate and fornicate with such a beautiful heroine that he once wanted to kill without compromise was an ease for his psyche. These days, he couldn't give anyone a real piece of his heart, but fucking was close. Violet could at least connect to him in that way.

They tried many positions. After unloading into Violet in a missionary session, Deadhead went for doggy style. With her hands subdued in handcuffs, Violet held onto the bed and took the cock as it fucked her deep in her anus. She came three times. Then, she rode him; legs spread and face looking up towards the sky. It would fulfill their evening together until 10 o'clock, their final orgasm shared. They could both tell that they had been satisfied. With all of that hard fucking, they had been given quite the exercise, and neither one of them could complain. After a hard session of fucking, Violet was ready to sleep, and Deadhead was ready to hit the streets again.

"Is it still stressful out there?" Violet said as she watched the villain zip up his suit. She was still naked.

"It's stressful to the average person. I was born for it." The villain tipped his head. "Until next time. Ta ta."

Leaving the room, Deadhead closed the door and headed back downstairs, leaving Violet to wonder just how much had changed since she left the crime-fighting scene. Not a lot, she hoped with honesty.

೫೪೦

Deadhead had never been a simple villain. With penetrating eyes and a fierce mind, he seemed to burn with arrogance. At a tall 6'6, it was hard to ignore how intimidating the man could be. His dark cape draped behind him everywhere he went—in alleyways, on rooftops, and in the midst of villain gatherings and meetings. The man always stood out. His black gloves and boots shined as his red suit held his emblem—a death's head staring rudely at anyone that crossed his path. Deadhead was the last villain that anyone would want to cross down a dark alley, let alone a superhero or heroine.

The first thing Deadhead learned as a budding supervillain was simple. Gaining respect in a circle of reputable criminals, the first thing his fellow villains told him was to trust no one, not even them. Those first days were very profitable. They made a great deal of money. Women followed, even molls that were willing to take the arm of a supervillain and bring chaos to the world. Many police were afraid to patrol the areas that supervillains chose as their haunts. The lifestyle they led brought them a lot of respect through the streets—or was it fear? Any wise citizen walked out of their way, knowing that even looking into one of their eyes could be incentive for their kneecaps to be broken. Many small-time criminals signed up to become henchmen and loyal goons, knowing that money was good under powerful, eccentric crime lords with funny costumes and weird names. Those days were good, very much so.

These days were even better for Deadhead. Once living in a time where he had a huge staff and loyal following, he was on his own now. As a solitary villain, he felt fulfilled. Deadhead always considered himself to be a misanthropic soul. God, he hated people! The look of them, the smell, the way they polluted the world. To Deadhead, humanity was a disease, and he would be the world's cure to humanity.

For some reason, as much as he hated people, however, Deadhead loved sex, and it was easy to come by. He had grown bored of having sex with regular women. Even loyal molls who would die for him, as many often did, didn't really do it for him. The only thing at the moment that truly satisfied his sexual lust was the fucking of a superheroine, embarrassing them by making them give in to the dark side. To have a heroine bent over, showing her ass or presenting her breasts for him, made the villain want to fuck even more of them. If he could ever make a heroine of the Big City's best superladies, he would do it. He even had a list for the many superheroines that he had fucked. There was Violet, of course, who was mediocre at best in his mind. Then there was the Mad Bullet Woman, Super Vox, The Green Beauty, and one of his favorites, The Scarlet Bird. Amongst those names, there were at least thirty or forty more, but sometimes, the villain lost count in his mind. For some reason, when many of them came to kill him, they would end up fucking. "Let's just cut to the chase," Deadhead would often say after the women had been tired in combat. It was simple. Deadhead had matured in his criminal career, and he knew just what the heroines wanted. It was all foreplay for real, explosive sex. The criminal wanted sex, drugs, and rock and roll. The heroine, in her warped thinking, thought that she wanted to pursue a life of morality and virtue, but that wasn't the case. What a heroine really wanted, and always wanted, was to join her pure sense of self with the dark perceptions they placed upon the villain. They wanted sex. They wanted to be had and used, fucked, and then get on with their lives without attachment. Nice guys finished last and the world of a villain brought chaos.

A lot of Deadhead's old buddies were gone now, either giving up on the criminal lifestyle, in jail, or dead. He had to admit it—when he was first going into the supervillain lifestyle, he assumed that everything would play out more like a comic book. Those were the days of naivety, a time when he was still recovering from drugs and trying to find a new hobby to become obsessed with. In the long run, everything proved to be more real than he could imagine. Deadhead had been through it all and the words of his early circle rang true. He couldn't trust anyone. He had employed goons that had tried to kill him and take over his territory, women that tried to poison him in his sleep and even officers disguised as criminal friends, trying to get leads. The pain of having to work with people was too much.

Going solo was the best thing that happened in Deadhead's villainous career. Sure, he didn't have the huge building that he used to hide out in and carry his operations, but then again, he never became a villain just for the money or even the

power. He became a villain because he knew
that he had a strong darkness within him,
one that made him different than any
regular person. It was his mission to spread
his inner chaos and negativity on the world.
He hated everything that was pure,
everything that stood for justice, peace, and
the sanity of humanity. In his mind, he was
the perfect villain of mankind. Most of his
old friends had stopped at gaining turf,
selling drugs, and creating strange
inventions aiming for world domination.
They always failed, eventually. Deadhead
survived them all. He knew the secret was
beyond such cliché desires for control. No,
the point was to have no control. To be wild.
To be free. That was what scared the world
more than anything, what made the true
super villain untouchable.

To the rest of the world, he would
probably be seen as a failure. He knew this.
He knew that people probably looked at old
photos and posters of him with a laugh. At
one point, he was being called the new
thing, the latest threat for the world to fear.
Documentaries and magazine articles dealt
strictly with him. Fools, all of them.
Deadhead was the greatest, and he always
would be.

That's right, you idiots, Deadhead
thought to himself proudly as he walked
down an alley in the slums, cloaked by
night. Forget about me. Think that I'm dead,
that I've lost, but remember that you haven't
seen the last of me. Not just yet.

Now, they wanted to kill him. Deadhead

laughed. If they wanted to come for him, let them come. That was his attitude about the whole matter. He didn't care who these individuals were or what they wanted. Anyway, he was going to dispose of any enemy that he had. Never did he care if they were going to come for him. He was ready. His powers were way more deadly, his expertise of combat highly evolved. Once the most feared member of his organization, he knew that no one had the balls to really take him on. Maybe a few would talk about it here and there, or set up operations like the little explosion near the restaurant that afternoon, but he really didn't fear any of them. They were all little punks as far as he was concerned. Deadhead felt like he had died numerous times before in his youth, being shot at by police or beaten up by superheroes, only to come back stronger than before and beat them all. As Big City's most recognized mastermind, he relished the day he could have a full on war with his old circle. They would regret it—that was a fact he was sure of.

His hand pressed against a steel door. Opening it, he walked into a room. It was quiet, filled with nothing but weapons and posters of naked heroines that he had personally taken. They were everywhere almost, except for first few feet of the room. In that nearly empty space, there was a small chair. It was where Deadhead liked to sit for a while, reliving a time that was gone and preparing for a time that was coming. He would remake the world in his own image; make his own world order. People would bow down and fear him. They would raise their hands and wish for him to bring them aboard for his new world order. In return for their pleading, their begging, and their pathetic want to live and to see another day, Deadhead would bless them with death. That was his mission in life—to kill. There could be no other way.

Deadhead sat down in the chair, pressing his hands against his knees. Preparing himself for meditation, he took in a deep breath, holding it before releasing it calmly. As he sat in the chair, he let his mind go. All of his thoughts emptied. His emotions seemed to not matter anymore. The world was slowly becoming less physical, dying in the background of silence. It was here that his perfect vision came into focus. Appealing to his nihilistic heart, meditation was what ready him to unleash chaos into the world.

ᚲᛞᛦᛂ

Deadhead and The Scarlet Bird fucked.

She was the bossy redhead. Her costume was a skintight yellow leotard, a white mask with matching white gloves and boots. She was about 5'9, slender yet noticeably muscular and strong. There were few things that intimidated Deadhead and The Scarlet Bird came pretty close to being one of them.

Whenever they came together, it was like the world was ending. With Scarlet dipping her head back, spreading her legs, and offering her full breasts into Deadhead's lips, the man felt like he was in control again. He didn't have to feed into the chaos that constantly drove him, or get lost in the rhythm of his own dark heart.

A part of him wanted to change. It really did. As much as he loved being evil, upsetting human order, and giving mankind trouble, he secretly wished to be normal. Ever since he was a petty criminal, he wondered why he had been made different from other human beings. What was the thing that drove him to create such negativity in the world? Why did he hate when he could see the love for life in the eyes of those around him, even the most down and out cynic? What caused him to have psychopathic and sociopathic tendencies that fueled his criminal career with an unrelenting fire? He didn't know, honestly. He felt like he would never really, truly know. Maybe he would always be lost in the world of pain that had been set for him before he was born. It was fate, destiny, the wheel turning with his lifeline setting the path for him.

Then there was The Scarlet Bird. She was a mystery that was unexplainable. With red hair that draped her shoulders and back like a fine silk scarf, she starred out with green eyes that seemed to hold a mystery. She smiled with red lips that were ruby, kissing Deadhead's cheek as he fucked her, wanting more. She begged for more. The gloved fingers that trailed against her skin excited her, made her vibrate in bed. She pushed her pussy against his cock, helping the villain as he forced it into her. He needed this.

She was in his lair. She had come here to fight with him. This always happened. He would cause a bunch of horrific crimes, scaring the world to death as they feared a nearing apocalypse. The only heroine humanity felt they could really trust would go to Deadhead's lair. She would go to save them, the people of the world, only to fuck this evil and chaotic fuck. Why?

Trust no one, Deadhead reasoned. Not even the closest villain. Why would it be different for a superheroine?

Deadhead didn't trust The Scarlet Bird, yet he fucked her. Every time they saw each other, they would fight for minutes, delivering powerful blows to each other, punching and kicking madly. They would get bruises, sometimes scars that would never heal, and black eyes. The woman could really carry her own and she was never afraid to fight a man. It didn't matter to her. She was going stand tough and tall.

He liked his women tough and The Scarlet Bird was the toughest of all, not like a vanilla sex fiend in the likes of a Violet or Green Beauty. She liked to be slapped. She loved being fucked hard and sucking on Deadhead's cock before it exploded in wads, sticking to her hair and her face. She even liked being spanked and tied up.

The season ended peacefully, even though it had gotten pretty violent in the beginning. Scarlet rode the villain's cock until he exploded and she exploded as well, their juices mixing before falling down on the ground and cradled in each other's arms.

They were in the woman's apartment. Only Deadhead knew The Scarlet Bird's secret identity. She was a lawyer, an attorney by day and a crime fighter by night. This night, however, she was taking the day off.

"I heard your old circle is coming to kill you."

Deadhead laughed. "I guess word gets around quickly, huh?"

"The explosion at the French restaurant was all over the news."

The villain fell silent.

Scarlet looked at the villain with sorrowful eyes, pressing her finger against his lips. "You know, you don't have to take on everything by yourself. Sure, we're enemies in our super personas. That doesn't mean that you can't get representation. Remember my occupation. I can get you into a witness protection program. You can rat on all of your old friends, get them arrested. I'll even represent you in court."

The villain laughed. "You really think that would work, don't you?"

The Scarlet Bird looked into his eyes, her own pupils wet and full of concern.

Deadhead shook his head. "You wouldn't believe the many crimes I have committed, Scarlet. I am a dark individual. I've done things that would never have me qualified for any program. I would be locked up and never released in public." Deadhead shook his head. "No. I have a great life out here and I'm not afraid of anyone. Besides, I wouldn't want you to get caught up in my problems. The public would be very suspicious with you as my lawyer. Don't full yourself."

Scarlet smiled. "You wouldn't want me mixed up in your problems? Is that a hint of concern there?"

The villain's face remained stone cold, yet his eyes bulged. Scarlet could sense discomfort in him from her words. She knew that the villain never wanted to be seen as caring.

"I've got to go," the villain said as he got up, searching for his clothes.

"Call me whenever you need a booty call, I guess," the heroine said calmly.

Without another word, the villain picked up his clothes and made it for the door.

Bam!

It had been simple. A sniper round to the back of the head. The fatal end of a high-rise criminal. There had been no huge warning, no big fight or even a moment of preparation. Just like that, Deadhead's career fell behind him and life faded.

The sniper had been parked outside of the attorney's apartment for quite a while. He knew the villain's huge ego and free movement around the city would make it easy to catch him off guard. More than anything, it was Deadhead's sexual appetite that would do him in. The villain's taste for sex could never be denied. After stalking him out for weeks on Mind Fiend's direction, he finally got a cohesive schedule down. For some reason, he really loved that attorney chick. It would be the end of him.

The sniper called his boss immediately, informing him that Deadhead was now officially dead.

"Excellent," Mind Fiend said over the phone. "You better get out of there. Hopefully no one saw you."

"No one," the sniper said with confidence. "Hey boss, you'll never believe what I found out while I was following this jerk for weeks."

"Go on."

"It seems the little bird he's been dating, well... I've been keeping an eye on her as well, since he goes there a lot. Seems that she's actually The Scarlet Bird."

"Ack! That bitch has been a problem for about a decade now. Come back to headquarters. We'll figure out a way to ruin her with this information."

"Wouldn't you rather just come back and wipe her out later?"

"No. It would be way more fun to see her reputation undo her. Much like that Plum Violet woman."

The sniper was always one to follow orders. After slipping out of the building, taking some back routes, and getting in his old sedan, the goon drove off quietly.

11 REALM OF THE DARK LADY

In the middle of a dark and mysterious forest in a faraway land, there was a lonely road. It was a gravelly road of dirt and rocks winding down a long path of trees that seemed to stretch so far into the sky; it was hard to see the extending branches that shot out from them. Very few people walked that road. There were many myths and folk legends dealing with the forest altogether— legends of ghosts, skeleton men, and other ghouls were said to haunt the woods. Scarier than anything else, however, was that dirt road. Most people would have rather run into a rotting corpse than to even touch one part of the path.

If one walked upon that dirt road, many things could happen to them, at least according to the legends of the people that lived near the woods. In most stories, the traveler would face certain death. If the person didn't die, according to other stories, the person would go entirely insane. Other stories said that the road would turn someone incredibly evil. The one thing that might have enticed someone to walk the road, however, was the more rare probability about the road. The least popular tales said that if one survived the calamities and dark energies of the road, they would find enlightenment. Very few people knew how to take that last one.

The road was said to be owned by the famous Dark Lady. It was said that only a great sage could see such a woman and live. The Dark Lady was the woman of the abyss, a lady that lived in the shadows of the world and created all of the alluring sights and sounds that a human being could get lost in. A woman of excellent beauty and poise, she was said to have long, dark hair and pale skin. She wore purple and carried crystals and stones with her. She was a being of the earth, and as such, she loved agriculture and growth. She protected the animals, the forests, and even the insects that crawled upon her territory. In her memory, she blessed the ones that could overcome the intoxicating thoughts and feelings of creation to find a peace beyond illusion. The ones that fell into her illusions, however, she punished. The people that lived near the forest believed that the Dark Lady existed and could travel anywhere, but the dirt path was specifically hers.

Throughout the centuries, different travelers would come to try to test the legends. As much as it scared the denizens of the lands, they couldn't help but be intrigued by these heroic figures that came to walk the mysterious path. They only came once every few decades or so, but somehow people would think that they could brave the roads and survive. There was the old mountaineer who came hundreds of years ago, bragging about his strength and lack of fear. It was easy to say that he was an impressive man. He felt like he could face anything and he didn't believe in ghosts and phantasms. After packing up and preparing for a trip down the dark path, he found himself engulfed beyond belief. When he came back, the people saw that his fears had claimed him. The man went mad.

Another man thought that he could survive the dark path. Only a few decades after the mountaineer, he went down the path and went searching for the Dark Lady. No one ever heard from him again. People felt it was safe to say that he died.

More and more people came. A surgeon, a knight, a survivalist... all types of different people from different backgrounds, occupations, and even social statuses, tried to survive the dark path and find out what was really there, and they had all failed. According to the town records, the only people that lived to survive and tell about the roads were the old sages who had come and gone over a millennium ago.

The townspeople thought about boarding up the road from the rest of the forest. Many were tired of hearing the stories of people dying. Others were afraid that phantasms from the other world travelled from the road and could harm them. For those fears, more churches were built and temples were prayed at. People built stone altars on the road to keep out the forces that they didn't understand, comprehend, or know how to deal with. All they knew was that they wanted to be free of the negativity that had been inflicted on their village and put a strange stigma on their way of life.

At one point and time, the ancestors of the people of the village had worshipped the Dark Lady. They saw her as a preserver of their village, a protector of their life stock, and the key to their survival. Unfortunately, the descendants saw the Dark Lady as a demon. They preached against her, spoke of her as a being of lust and death. Any old statues that were found of her were immediately broken. People prayed that she would be destroyed by other deities.

Still, the Dark Lady's energy was still around. It was as if the people couldn't get rid of her. All attempts to close down the road she owned were given up. The dirt road was still unblocked and the people of the village just decided to stay away from it. The technology of agriculture and farming was always changing and growing for the townspeople. They weren't as advanced as the rest of the world, probably. It would even be safe to say that a lot of them couldn't exist outside of the familiar and natural world that existed within the woods and fields. That was just fine with them. As long as they didn't have to suffer the wrath of the strange and enigmatic Dark Lady, their woodsy environment could possibly be enough.

One day, a man came from the east. His name was Hans. He had heard about the path and thought that he would see it for himself.

Hans was a simple man. He didn't labor too hard in life, but he was very fit and robust. Growing up in another farming town, he didn't get to hear a lot of different legends and fables growing up. If anything, Hans had always thought that his life was quite boring. Hans liked life, and he liked people. He loved to learn from people and see what they had acquired in their travels. As far as how he knew himself, however, Hans felt like he hadn't traveled enough to have bragging rights in order to help someone acquire a worldly sense. That was why Hans planned to get as much travelling time in his adult life as possible. What would be better than to live and say he had walked the path that many were afraid to tread—the path of the Dark Lady?

Walking into the town, Hans truly felt like a stranger. Never in his life had he felt so different from anyone in his life. It was as if he was walking in a dream. He saw people doing things that he was used to seeing in his village—cooking, cleaning, building houses, getting crops, gardening, and other things. Still, their disposition was different. The townspeople were Hans was from were usually cheery and upbeat. They sang songs while they worked. These people sang and said nothing. They went from chore to chore, literally looking like the living dead. Their faces seemed to be drained of any real mirth or enjoyment. Hans couldn't help but find it sad. He was hoping that coming to the village would be a real opportunity to meet some good friends or see some good sights, and all he saw was a living ghost town.

Hans stopped a man on the road.

"Excuse me," Hans asked politely. "Do you know where I can find the path of the Dark Lady?

The man gasped, looking as if he had seen death. "Hey... surely, you do not plan on walking down that road?"

Hans grinned wildly. "Yes. I've been preparing for that road for a while now. I've wanted to do this for a long time."

The man shook his head. "Crazy man. You would be better forgetting all about that road and going back wherever you came from."

Hans laughed. What a weakling! This man surely was ruled heavily by fear. "What are you so afraid of, man? It's just a road."

The man shook his head. "Yeah. Yeah, you think it's just a road. Just you wait and see. It's not just a road. If you think you can just get on the road and walk off, you've got another thing coming. Once you get on that road, you're on it forever."

Hans rolled his eyes. "Yeah, man. I am the type of person that has to find things out for myself. I can't really do that with you pushing your strange fears on me. Good bye."

The man watched Hans as he started to walk off. "Good bye."

Turning down the way he came, Hans looked around for an entry into the forest. He was tired of the village. He thought that he would go and stay at the inn, sleep for a while and then set out but he didn't want to stay there any longer. The place was far too neurotic for him. He would be better off camping in the woods.

The trees were better company than the people had been, that was for sure. The trees stretched up high to the sky. Hans had never seen anything like it. He truly felt alone in the world.

Hans wasn't much of a navigator. He had followed his map well enough to know how to get to the village but he didn't really know how to get to the path in the forest. He would have to walk around a little bit. The place looked pretty well maintained. There were road markers to indicate where everything was just in case he got lost. Hans didn't know if there would be a sign to show exactly where the path would be or not, but he would keep an eye out for anything that looked out of the ordinary.

His answer was soon answered. He saw a sign that said "Path of the Dark Lady—one mile ahead."

He could feel his heart beating. Could it be that the famed path truly did exist? Would he really get a chance to walk on it? There was a high sense of elation. He could just cherish being that close to discovering it. Still, he kept his mind focused on the prize. No, he came here for the path, he reminded himself. Don't get so excited so soon—there was still more of a way to go.

Hans stayed on the path without a want to stray. He felt so close to his goal. At times, he felt tired, and contemplated sleep, but he knew he came way too far to give up now. There was no way he was going to turn back around to that dead husk of a village and see those people again. He wasn't ready to set up camp, even as the sky had grown dark. Hans knew that he wanted to see the Dark Lady in the night anyway, to know her power and embrace who she was as her true form.

His legs were getting tired. It wasn't the mile that had done it. Hans had been travelling all day. In his excitement, he hadn't paid attention to any fatigue. After the disappointment of the area's people, however, he couldn't help but notice his body's need for rest. Still, he fought it. No—the mystery was far more important than a temporary feeling of being tired.

Suddenly, Hans had to wipe his eyes in disbelief. Standing before him, cutting through a path in the forest, was a road of dirt and rock gravel. A sign in front of the road said "Path of the Dark Lady."

Hans stared at the road with a chuckle. "This is it? This is the big, bad road?"

A big, howling gust of wind blew in Han's face from the road, as if giving him an invitation. Hans could feel a strange gravitational pull from the road that he couldn't describe as well. Looking at the sky, Hans smiled as he saw that it was finally night time.

"So," Hans said as he stood in front of the road, taking in a deep breath before letting it out calmly and slowly. "I'm here."

Hans stepped on the road. Looking forward, he stared into the night air of the path, feeling the gravel under his feet. He heard the squishing noises of his shoes and could feel the rocky texture with little protection. Marching on, Hans looked up at the trees and realized that he couldn't even see the sky anymore.

The wind howled. It was cold and the air was damp. As dark and grave as everything seemed, there was a beauty in it all. Hans didn't really feel afraid of the road or even cautious of it. If anything, he was sure that it was completely safe. There was nothing odd looking about the route or even attractive outside of its simple nature. The dirt road seemed just like any other dirt road. Thinking on the superstitions he had heard before coming there, Hans just laughed at the stupidity of human beings.

"How quick people are to believe in ghost, phantasms, and unexplained phenomenon based on fairy tales," Hans said before laughing to himself. "Unbelievable."

At the same time, Hans was a bit disappointed and kind of sad. He wanted to have a weird and crazy experience happen to him. Hans was looking forward to meeting the Dark Lady. He had really convinced himself that she existed. Maybe she would grant him some favor, give him a gift for looking for her. She was the queen of nature, wasn't she? Maybe she would have told Hans some secret that only special people could know, the people that lived to stand face to face with the Goddess and tell about it. It seemed like that wasn't going to be.

Hans had to have been walking for 15 minutes by now.

"If things keep going this way," Hans thought to himself, "I'm going to wind up in some forgotten village or something. Or maybe I'll just see another side of the forest those ignorant villagers were too chicken to find." With that, Hans laughed again.

The winds continued to blow. The trees swayed in the breeze even though their high ends were nearly invisible, melded with the heights of the night. Hans had to reach into his belongings and pull out a lantern. Taking a stop, he lit it up and made sure that the flame burned bright. After he secured the flame in the lantern, Hans was off to walk once again.

It was at that moment that a strong wind blew out the flame.

Hans stared at his lantern in amusement. Isn't that funny, Hans thought. Well, either he would again attempt to light the lantern or he would just stumble in the dark. His hand went for the matches that were in his belongings. Kneeling down, Hans prepared to get the lantern glowing.

The wind increased again. Suddenly, the lantern flew out of his hands along with the matches. The lantern broke into pieces with the matches scattered all over the ground.

"Fuck!" Hans called out as the darkness enveloped him.

Suddenly, a strong bright white light shot out at Hans.

Hans got scared. "What the fuck is this?"

Hans stared out in the dark to see the bright light shining. It was at the very edge of the path, yards away. A strong feeling of dread and fear entered Han's gut as he wasn't sure what was happening now. He felt like a fly that had been caught in a trap, his thoughts slowly disintegrating in the heat of this light burning through him, changing him forever.

Hans took a moment to look around the light. All around the light were lower beings—demons, flying things, screaming things that didn't know how to embrace the light that was the nucleus on the path. Hans suddenly became afraid that he could disappear easily, being eaten or destroyed by one of these weird and fantastical beings. Covering his head, Hans hoped that the weird beings would go away and that he could survive.

Wanting to edge near the light, Hans would have to wait. For now, Hans felt frozen in place. He would not be allowed to move any further. Like a fly, he was trapped, forced to endure the energy of an unintelligible light that felt like it was trying to eat him. Hans didn't know if he should trust and focus on the light of the path or just give up and be eaten by the dark beings around it.

No, he thought. That's how they go crazy, he thought. I know now. That is how they go crazy. They focus on the illusions.

Hans gained control. He wouldn't focus on the demons. He wouldn't focus on the light. He would just allow everything to be as it naturally existed. There was no need to battle between phantasms and projections. Whatever needed to come would come. Whatever was going to happen to Hans, it was going to happen. There was no need to try to stop or deny anything now.

With that realization, Hans grew increasingly scared. His reasoning made absolute sense, but he didn't trust his mind's ability to let go of things and just be, or exist. It all scared him to no end and a part of him wanted to die right then and there.

He felt another, stronger part of his being as well. Within his heart, blaring, trumpeting, was a strong need and desire to live. Yes, he would survive this. He would live. His feet dug into the earth below him, holding his place.

The demons blared past him. Darkness and light shattered. Suddenly, Hans was standing in the center of what seemed to be night and day, all at once. The forest and even the world seemed to disappear. All he could see before him that was real was a woman that was glowing in front of him. Her hair was dark, her skin pale, and her clothes purple. Immediately, she stripped herself of her garments and started to walk forward.

"The Dark Lady," Hans recognized without confusion.

The woman started to walk forward, smiling as she noticed Hans looking at her.

"Yes, I am her. I am the Dark Lady that you seek."

Hans felt his eyes open wide. "I did it. I did it! I made it! I survived!"

The Dark Lady nodded. "Yes. You did. Congratulations."

Hans shook his head. "So you are it. You're the goddess of our Earth? The Dark? I'm so confused."

"I am whatever people want me to be," the woman said as she slipped into Han's arms and gave him a deep, passionate kiss. From then on, there would be no more questions.

Hans grabbed the woman in his arms and pressed his lips against hers. She had a very soft and gentle kiss, not too forceful at all. It felt just right. She rubbed Hans' arms passionately as if he were her husband. Hans felt himself getting hard in his pants, wanting to fuck the Dark Lady so bad. A tear dropped down his cheek. Around any other woman, Hans would have been afraid to cry. In front of the Dark Lady, however, it felt like nothing but the best thing to do.

"Allow me to take you into my arms and give you pleasure, dear," the woman said to him.

Hans moaned as he leaned into the Dark Lady's breasts. "Yes, please."

Obediently, Hans held the woman close as she kissed him up and down his neck.

The Dark Lady teased his ear, biting on it and pulling it. Hans had sprung in his pants immediately. He could only smile as the Dark Lady started to help him strip, dropping his pants and pulling off his shirt. When his shoes and pants had been thrown to the side and the man was just as nude as the Dark Lady, he felt free. Hans forgot about anything holding him back—his old town, his name, even his thoughts and belief system. All that existed now was him and the goddess—there was no need to worry about anything trivial or wasteful.

The two got back to kissing. In their long and sensual kiss session, lips were teased, tongues were flipped and lunged, and hands held each other tight. They kept each other in place. Hans wondered if this moment was similar to what the first male and female went through when they came to Earth.

Hans felt his cock brush against the Dark Lady's cunt. Before long, she was helping him stab her with his hard cock. Hans slammed the cock into her pussy, which fit the woman perfectly. It was as if she was made for him.

"Only a few lucky ones have been able to make it this far," the Dark Lady said before she resumed her moaning and groaning from the pleasure of being united with the human.

"Yes, I know," Hans said.

"You heard the legends." Dark Lady smiled. "I see. That's why you came to pursuit me."

Hans nodded as he slowly worked his

cock into the Dark Lady's cunt, in and out, pushing it hard. "Yes."

The Dark Lady groaned as she felt her pussy being manhandled by this human. She loved it. Inside of her body, she could feel her feminine juices bubbling out of her cunt. She was dripping all over Hans, making him work his cock harder into her as she leaned against empty space. This was her realm, the void, deep within the Earth, within the Universe, within space—within everything.

Hans just gave in. He let himself melt, become of the Dark Lady that he was lusting more and more. His balls swung back and forth with each hard thrust. He held the woman down, grabbing her ass with strong hands, wanting to keep her close to him. God, she smelled so good, he thought. She had the scent of incense, or some sort of earthy midst. He couldn't put his finger on it. Whatever it was, he was sure that it was divine. It had to be. It was on her.

"Goddess, take my cock," Hans said sacrificially.

"Yes... give it to me," the Dark Lady said, taking her fucking like a champ.

Hans pressed the woman's wrists down, restraining her from moving too much as he did his duty. He wanted to do her the right way, the respectable way that a goddess should have sex. Going missionary was the main thing that popped in his head. He couldn't stomach the thought of treating the woman like any random human lady. Fucking her deeply, he didn't even notice that they were swimming and fucking in space, galaxies, and comets in the background.

The goddess screamed, her pussy dripping onto the ground, spraying on Hans with each thrust. Her own cum could revitalize a ground suffering from drought. The very tears that came out of her eyes could restore a dying flower.

God, Hans thought with intrigue, let me make her happy, please. He was making her very pleased, even with his worry and fear. Hans was making the woman cream for him and she gives her life's substance to his cock. She was giving him a new existence, a new awakening.

As they came together, the goddess and the human hugged for a long time. They rolled over and watched the stars and comets roll across the sky.

Epilogue

The people of the village continue to fear the path. It is a path that is rarely traveled. Most are fully convinced that the road brings sorrow, travesty, and pain. Others believe there is a slim chance that it can bring enlightenment.

Very few people take the step to test the theory. In a fear of dying or going insane, they stay sheltered in the protection of their villages and communities, waiting for things to blow over. They work to stay normal, to have people respect them and never go outside the wall. Thinking outside of the box can be dangerous for most.

But there is a possibility that for the few,

there can be more to gain. Yes, for the few, there may be a way to find something on the road scarier than fear, death, insanity, and chaos. In the complexities and intricate workings of life, there may be a simple road that leads to full and absolute peace.

Since few take that road, who truly knows?

AUTHOR'S NOTE

Readers: I want to expand a few of the stories to see where the characters can be explored further. If there are any of the stories that you would like to read more about again, I'd love to hear from you!

Visit my blog at www.parkerheimann.com

Join my newsletter for free exclusive previews
http://www.parkerheimann.com/in

Follow me on Twitter at
http://www.twitter.com/parkerheimann

Like my page on Facebook at
http://www.facebook.com/parkerheimann

Discover my books at major ebook retailers everywhere.